BETTER THAN GOLD

THERESA TOMLINSON

A & C BLACK
AN IMPRINT OF BLOOMSBURY
LONDON   NEW DELHI   NEW YORK   SYDNEY

They let the ground keep that precious treasure,
Gold under gravel, gone to earth,
Useless to men now as it ever was.

(From the Anglo-Saxon poem *Beowulf*)

The following story is inspired by real people, places
and events. However, some names, locations and dates
have been changed, as have certain descriptive details.
Some events and characters are completely fictional.

Contents

Chapter 1	Faint-heart's Brat!	7
Chapter 2	Sacrifice to Woden	14
Chapter 3	The Lucky One	22
Chapter 4	The Pagan Queen	29
Chapter 5	Queen's Court	36
Chapter 6	Queen's Boon	43
Chapter 7	Another Familiar Face	51
Chapter 8	The World Turned Upside Down	60
Chapter 9	Peace	68
Chapter 10	A Battle of Words	75
Chapter 11	A Coward's Act	83
Chapter 12	War	90
Chapter 13	King's Gold	99
Chapter 14	Blood-month	108
Chapter 15	Woden's Man	117

CHAPTER 1

Faint-heart's Brat!

B rother Chad strode into the chamber, waving the knife that usually swung at his belt. It dripped with blood. Egfrid leapt to his feet, shocked to see his young book-master's habit bloodied and torn.

'What has happened?' he cried.

Annis, his nurse, looked up startled and put down the bowl of oatmeal she prepared. 'Are you hurt, Brother Chad?' she cried.

'Not *my* blood,' he said. 'We must get the boy out of here! Mercians have got in through the outer gate.'

'No,' she cried. 'That cannot happen!'

'But it *has* happened. This is Mercian blood on my blade and the gate-warden is dead. The guards were slaughtered while they slept and the gate stands open. They'll be here in no time.'

The way they spoke over his head, taking no notice of him, made Egfrid angry. He snatched up the light practice sword that hung from a hook on the wall and waved it. 'I'll go out and do battle,' he cried.

'Have you a skirt that might fit him?' the monk asked, continuing to ignore the boy.

Annis began to pull old gowns from a chest. 'These were his sister's, when she was young, but…'

'Too rich,' Chad shook his head. 'We need plain stuff—the cook's daughter perhaps?'

'No time!' Annis cried, throwing up her hands in despair. 'No time, you said!'

They were silent for a moment, but then she snatched up the gown on the top of the chest and began to rip at the tablet-weave braid that edged the sleeves and neckline. 'You wanted plain,' she muttered.

Without another word the monk wrenched the sword from Egfrid and dragged the boy's burnished leather tunic up and over his head. 'I'm sorry, my prince, no time for gentleness!' he said.

Egfrid was shocked by this rough treatment, from those who were usually kind to him. They thrust him into his sister's old gown, now ragged at the edges.

'Cover his head!' said Chad.

'No,' Egfrid protested. 'I'm ten years old! I'm no girl and will not dress like one.'

But Annis ripped another piece of cloth and Brother Chad held him firmly, while she fastened a makeshift kerchief tightly about his head.

'No, no, no!' he cried, twisting and turning in their grip.

Screams and shouts came from the courtyard below, followed by the thunder of booted feet on the stairs. The monk and nurse exchanged a terror-filled glance. Brother Chad made the Christian sign, *three-gods-in-one*, and then the door crashed open and two warriors burst in on them, swords drawn and bloody.

The monk stepped in front of Egfrid, meat knife at the ready, but a red-faced giant of a man stumped into the chamber. He raised his fist, and sent knife and monk skittering helplessly across the floor. The giant was old with white hair and beard, and dragged his leg a little when he walked, but he was broadly-built and fearless. 'Who is this maid that you defend so bravely, holy man?' he growled.

Egfrid tore the kerchief from his head and snatched up the monk's discarded knife. 'I'm no maid.' He drew himself straight with a pride that matched the old warrior's. 'I am Egfrid, son of King Oswy Iding, and my father will kill you for attacking my book-master.'

The Mercians laughed. Egfrid lunged at the giant, but the man's great fist came down fast again. The boy fell, knocked to the floor by the blow. He gasped, but still managed to cry out in anger. 'You will be cursed by the Christ-God for this.'

'Blessed Woden!' the giant said, and a slow smile spread across his face. 'We have Oswy's brat and they've dressed him in women's weeds! Shall we call him Lady Faint-heart?' He threw back his head and roared with laughter.

Egfrid's courage fled as he saw that he'd given himself away.

'Do you know who I am, boy?' the giant bellowed. 'I am Penda, king of the Mercians—your father's greatest enemy. I am the nightmare of your dreams! Bind him hand and foot and take him down to Thunderer! Burn this place! Oswy Iding will never dare leave home again!'

One of the men grabbed Egfrid. He roped the boy's hands behind his back and tied his feet. Then he picked him up and threw him over his shoulder as though he were a trussed deer. The Mercians shouted to each other as Egfrid was jolted down the stairs.

'Treasure?' one asked.

'Treasure of sorts,' was the reply. 'We've got the Faint-heart's brat! Better than gold, he is!'

This was greeted by wild laughter and shield beating.

The Mercians had sneaked in from the south while Egfrid's father was away gathering tribute from the Pictish king and his mother visiting a holy woman, two days' ride to the north. It was no new thing for the Mercians to come raiding, but the fortress of Bamburgh, built high on its great rock above the sea, was believed to be impregnable.

Egfrid was carried down into the outer court. He tried not to look at the piles of bodies strewn there, and the rumpled, bloodstained clothing of the cook and her daughter.

Penda's men hacked at the stalls and livestock pens that filled the space. They dragged wood towards the great hall and, scattering fowls and frightened sheep, they built a pyre about his home. Dogs howled. Where was Woodruff, his favourite hound? Egfrid opened his mouth to call him, but closed it just in time, understanding that he'd call the loyal creature to his death.

Firebrands were carried from the kitchens and the stacks set ablaze. Screams and moans rose around him. Surely this could not be happening. It must be some frightful dream.

But then angry cries of surprise came from the Mercians—and even from his awkward position, Egfrid sensed his enemy's bewilderment. Had his father returned in time to rescue him? But no—thick smoke made him cough. The wind had changed direction and sent the flames back into the faces of the men who'd lit them.

'Mount up!' Penda shouted. He struggled to climb into the saddle himself, but as soon as he'd managed it he pointed to Egfrid. 'Give me my treasure!'

The boy was thrown over the saddle of Penda's horse, where he slumped face down, rump in the air, across the giant's saddle.

'Get out! Leave them to burn!' Penda bellowed.

Egfrid lifted his head and shouted, 'The Christ-God has sent this wind to punish you!' The changing wind had come from Aidan's Isle—the offshore monastery that Chad came from.

'Shut up!' He received a brutal thump across his ear from the man who'd carried him.

Penda took the reins and wheeled his stallion about. 'We have what we came for,' he cried, 'something to make the Faint-heart weep! Cease your whining, boy, and prepare for the ride of your life!'

CHAPTER 2
Sacrifice to Woden

Egfrid wanted to die. Every part of his body was battered and bruised. The Mercians galloped south, scattering flocks, swinging spears and swords at man or beast that got in their way. These men were pagans who worshipped Woden and Thunor the thunder-god. They made horrible blood sacrifices and he was terribly afraid that they meant to sacrifice him.

Penda stopped at noon in a small village that they terrorised with threats and demands. The poor inhabitants ran to bring bread, cheese, smoked pigs' haunches and their best ale. After another brief rest they rode southwards again and Egfrid fell into a deep, creeping misery. When darkness came, they stopped again, throwing the boy into a patch of heather. He lay helpless as the men rushed to assist Penda down from his horse.

Egfrid shut his eyes and prayed that he'd wake to find he'd been riding the nightmare. If his father heard how he'd opened his mouth and stupidly given himself away, there'd be little sympathy from him for his plight. What a fool he'd been. He must pay dearly now, for one moment of mad pride. Why, oh why had he not meekly obeyed Brother Chad and pretended to be a servant girl?

His mother, Queen Eanfleda, would weep when she heard he'd been taken. She'd order monks and nuns to pray for him and give more gold to the churches, hoping the Christ-God would save him, but Egfrid had little hope that anyone could save him now. He'd lost everything—his home, his pony, his hounds, his proud status as a royal prince.

A tiny scrap of comfort floated through the darkness when he thought he heard Annis calling to him. 'I'm here, Egfrid… Annis is here.'

Then the sound grew muffled, as though the Mercians had shut her up. His own ear throbbed painfully from the blow he'd received. Would they hit Annis, too? She'd called out the gentle words she'd used to comfort him when he was small. 'I'm here… Annis is here,' she'd cry, when he fell or banged his head.

She'd soothe his wounds with marigold balm and somehow put things right again—but she could do nothing for him now.

He guessed they must be heading for Deira, towards his father's cousin's palace at York, but there was little chance that Oswin Yffi would ride out to save him. His father's handsome young cousin was known as Oswin the Good, for he was a very Christian king, but he only ruled these lands with Penda's consent and an annual payment of gold and grain.

Egfrid's father had wanted Deira for himself. He sneeringly called his young rival 'Oswin the Perfect'.

One of the men brought a horn of strong-smelling mead to Penda and he took a long drink. He smacked his lips and said with a chuckle, 'Give our little lady a sip!'

When the boy turned his head away, Penda reached out to grab him brutally by the hair and tip his head back. 'Drink!' he ordered.

Egfrid was forced to gulp down the powerful stuff and some of it slopped onto the shameful gown that he still wore. 'You're a fool, just like your father,' Penda growled. 'This will help you bear the journey, for we must ride fast.'

Egfrid looked away and thought that he saw two men that he recognised wandering freely amongst the Mercians. They usually rode with his cousin Prince Ethelwald. What were they doing in the company of raiders?

Then one of them looked at him and smiled; a sneering smile and Egfrid understood. Chad had said that the gates were open, and the guards slaughtered. These men had betrayed him. They were in Penda's pay. Dark rage rose against them—he'd kill them if he could, but the mead he'd been forced to drink took effect and soon, despite himself, he slept.

He was roused at daybreak, made to drink mead again, and once more thrown across the king's saddle. His thoughts grew muddled and his eyes drooped, so that he no longer felt the bumping pain of the stallion's gallop. Darkness closed in on him as though it was still night.

Day and night merged together and Egfrid was only vaguely aware of more stops, more drinks of mead that he gulped down, welcoming the warm darkness that it brought. When he eventually came to his senses again, he opened his eyes to find that he was looking dizzily down into bright waters, which crept ever closer to his face. Sun warmed the back of his head, while the animal scent of the stallion filled his nostrils and he discovered that he felt sick. As the water came closer still, he wondered if they were going to drown him.

Penda's sturdy mount ploughed on. Soon Egfrid's face was splashed, there was a taste of mud in his mouth, and he had a dim understanding that they were crossing a wide river. Could it be the River Humber, which marked the southern boundary of Deira? His heart sank at the thought, for once across it, he could never hope to escape.

The water receded as the stallion moved through shallows and out onto marshy ground. Egfrid's stomach heaved. He opened his mouth and vomited down the rippling muscular shoulder of the horse.

This involuntary action was greeted with a roar of disapproval from Penda. 'Damn me, by Woden's teeth, the brat has spewed. Call a halt! Now that we're free of Faint-heart's lands, we'll rest the beasts and ride on through the night.'

Shouts and orders travelled down the line and the horses were hobbled and set free to graze in the meadows that lined the river bank. Penda dismounted with difficulty and sat down on a rock. Egfrid was hauled down after him.

'Sit him up beside me,' Penda ordered. 'He has a right to see how we deal with those who betrayed him.'

So Egfrid was propped up beside the king.

'Fetch Ethelwald's men for their just reward!' the king growled.

Egfrid looked with hatred at the two that he'd recognised earlier, but at Penda's brief nod, they were grabbed from behind and disarmed.

'Take them to yonder ash tree, slit their throats and hang them by their feet, as a sacrifice to Woden,' the king ordered.

Egfrid gasped in astonishment, while the two men collapsed, begging pitifully for their lives.

But Penda was merciless. 'They're traitors to their kind and death is all they deserve,' he said. 'Now bring the other captives here.'

The men were dragged away to their fate, leaving Egfrid shaken. He shut his eyes, not wishing to witness his betrayers' miserable deaths, but Penda had other ideas.

'Open your eyes,' he bawled.

When Egfrid obeyed he saw that Annis and Brother Chad had been dragged forwards, both of them bound hand and foot as he was. They were forced to kneel in the mud, looking pale and dirty, but both stared calmly into the distance, refusing to plead.

'See who we have here,' Penda said, as though Egfrid were a fool, or a little child. 'Your holy man and little mother-hen!'

Egfrid nodded miserably.

'Swear that you will not try to escape, and you will be set free from these bonds. But if you break your word, these two shall be Woden's next sacrifice.'

Egfrid's stomach churned at the thought of the ash tree and he nodded quickly. 'I agree,' he said.

'Swear by your god!'

'I swear by the Christ-God,' he said.

'Good,' said Penda. 'Take them away.'

Annis and Brother Chad were hauled away and though their mouths were not gagged, they suffered the indignity in silence.

'Unbind the boy!' Penda ordered.

Two warriors bent to release Egfrid's hands and ankles, but when they set him upright, he fell straight down again. He could see his feet and legs, but couldn't feel them.

'Rub his ankles, you fools,' Penda growled. 'Where is Fritha? Fetch the herb-wench!'

One of the warriors stooped awkwardly to pull off Egfrid's boots. A weather-beaten woman, dressed strangely in riding breeches and a man's short tunic, pushed her way through to them. Small bundles and vials swung from her belt.

'Get him standing straight for me!' Penda ordered. 'I want this trophy live and walking.'

'Out of the way then,' Fritha said. 'His bonds were knotted far too tight.'

CHAPTER 3
The Lucky One

Fritha started rubbing Egfrid's feet and ankles and it wasn't long before he began to feel a faint prickling sensation.

'Oooh,' he gasped.

She chuckled, and paused to unstop a vial, from which she poured some sharp-smelling oil. She worked it in to his skin. The sensation of tingling heat became overpowering.

'Oooh,' he gasped again.

He'd have liked to suffer in silence like Annis and Chad, but didn't seem able to manage it. The sensation was unpleasant, but vaguely familiar and he recognised that it must be gone through, in order for his feet to recover.

'Twitch your toes!' Fritha ordered.

The discomfort began to ebb and he found that he could wriggle his toes again.

'Can he stand and walk?' Penda asked.

Two men hauled him to his feet and this time he managed to stay upright. He took a shaky step, relieved that he could still walk, but a worrying thought came to him. Were Annis and Chad too tightly bound?

Penda watched him closely. 'How old are you?' he asked.

'I've seen ten summers,' Egfrid replied.

'Ten! Old enough to be fostered! They keep you coddled at home with a nurse, like a lass!'

Egfrid considered his life to be far from coddled. He was forced to spend hours learning to read and write, under Brother Chad's strict instruction. He longed instead to ride at his father King Oswy's side; to move from thane's hall to thane's hall to gather payment; to put down rebellion and pass judgement on those who'd broken the king's laws. Egfrid rarely saw his mother, for Queen Eanfleda spent most of her time visiting holy women and monasteries.

'My father seeks a foster family,' he said. 'But I need a royal household, as I am a king's son.'

Penda frowned. '*My* boy Wulfhere is fostered by the finest fighter in Mercia. I make my sons into warriors.' He rubbed his long white beard, watching Egfrid thoughtfully. At last he turned away. 'Fetch food,' he ordered. 'I could eat a horse!'

Egfrid sat on a rock and pulled on his boots. When the food came he accepted bread and cheese, and found that he was very hungry. Fritha sat down beside him to eat.

'You're the lucky one,' she said quietly.

Egfrid stared at her amazed; he'd been dragged from his home, carried far away, treated roughly and threatened with bloody pagan rites! How could he be lucky?

She chuckled, when she saw his expression. 'I know him,' she insisted. 'He likes the way you answer him. You live, don't you? The braver you are, the better he'll like you!'

Egfrid considered this.

'Is he wounded?' he asked.

'An old leg wound troubles him,' Fritha said, 'but no wound will keep Penda down.'

Egfrid ate, trying not to look in the direction of the ash tree. When drinks were offered he refused the mead, but accepted a sip of ale. Fritha saw how awkwardly he pulled at the neck of his sister's gown and searched in her baggage. She pulled out a worn pair of breeches and a rough tunic.

'Here,' she said. 'If you roll up the sleeves and legs, they'll fit you well enough.'

Egfrid struggled gratefully into them.

Penda's men dozed for a while by the river bank, but the king stumped back to his horse. 'Get moving,' he bellowed. 'Throw the lad up to me.'

Egfrid found himself seated astride Penda's stallion, in front of the king. He clutched at the thick dark mane of the powerful beast, and gently patted the muscular shoulder.

Penda saw the small gesture. 'His name is Thunderer. Can you stay upright, if we gallop?' he asked.

Egfrid remembered what Fritha had said. 'Yes,' he replied firmly. 'But can my book-master and nurse be released? They won't escape, for they'd never leave me.'

'Their lives are in your hands,' Penda said. 'We ride towards the backbone hills, and if you ride like a man, with no complaints, then your people will be freed from their bonds in the morning.'

Egfrid swallowed hard. 'But if their bonds are as tight as mine were, they might never walk again!'

There was a tense moment of silence, then Penda called for Fritha. 'Go back to the captives and see their feet untied, so they can ride upright. Not their hands, mind!'

Fritha raised an eyebrow at Egfrid and went off to find Chad and Annis.

'We head for Tamworth. Hold tight, boy!' Penda bellowed.

They headed south-west and at times Egfrid grabbed Thunderer's mane, to prevent himself from flying straight over the stallion's ears, but he was more comfortable riding upright. It grew dark, but Penda and his warriors knew the tracks well. Egfrid's heart leapt as they jumped a ditch and Penda's tree-trunk arms encircled him. He'd longed to ride with his father like this, but his mother declared it too dangerous. Perhaps he had been coddled a little!

All through the night they rode, stopping briefly to let the horses feed and rest. At last they moved through a high hill pass and as the ground began to slope downhill, an air of celebration developed. The warriors sounded their horns as they came to halt beside a rune-carved boundary stone.

'From here on all the land is mine,' Penda announced.

They dismounted and Egfrid found that he ached more than ever.

'I've not caused trouble,' he said, anxious that the king might forget his promise. 'I haven't complained!'

Penda gave a snort of amusement. 'Fetch the captives,' he ordered.

Annis and Chad appeared, more dishevelled than ever, a livid bruise on the nurse's mouth. Chad's chin and forehead were covered with stubble, for he usually shaved both, as his religion demanded. One of his eyes had turned black.

'Untie them,' Penda ordered.

Egfrid rushed to hug Annis.

'Dear boy,' she murmured softly. Then she sniffed at his tunic. 'What have they dressed you in?'

Egfrid grinned. 'I stink, don't I? But I'm content. Better than a lass's gown!'

She looked dismayed. 'We meant only to—'

'I know,' he cut in. 'You meant to save me and I should have listened to you.'

'Give them food and drink!' Penda ordered. 'But hear this, holy man: if you or the woman run, the boy will be killed instantly.'

Egfrid paled at the harsh words.

'We will not run,' Chad said quietly.

CHAPTER 4
The Pagan Queen

Two sturdy ponies were brought for Chad and Annis to ride.

'Not far to Tamworth,' Penda said. 'Hah! Wait till my queen hears that I've stolen Faint-heart Oswy's brat, she'll give me earache.'

'Why do you call my father Faint-heart?' Egfrid dared to ask.

Penda snorted with laughter as they set off again.

'Whenever I come north, he hides in some fortress. He never comes out to fight like his brother did. There was a man worth fighting. Oswald Whiteblade was no faint-heart.'

'But you killed him. You killed my uncle!'

Penda grunted. 'I killed him in battle. He died an honourable death. No warrior can ask more. A king must fight for his land, or he has no honour. Were Whiteblade still a worshipper of Woden, he'd have gone straight to the feasting hall of the gods. Your father is a coward who'll die in his bed!'

Egfrid bit his tongue, afraid to say more.

Penda kicked Thunderer into a gallop and Egfrid clung on tight, wishing he'd been brave enough to remind Penda what had happened after the battle in which Oswald Whiteblade was killed.

Egfrid's father never spoke of it, but Cedric, the oldest of his hearth-companions, had related the tale. He told how Oswy had ridden south, with only his closest companions, as soon as he heard of his brother's death. He'd discovered the battlefield and found Whiteblade's body, his head and arms set up on stakes, for a raven-feast.

Oswy, looking grim as death, had gathered his brother's remains, and carried them back to Bamburgh. That was surely no coward's act. But since then Oswy had been forced to submit to Penda's will, ruling only the northern part of his brother's kingdom.

Egfrid knew that he should hate this ruthless

old warrior. If he managed to survive and grow to manhood, he should try to kill him, but he also found that he could not forget the traitorous gate guards' terrible fate. There was something in Penda's startling sense of justice that made him hard to hate.

The countryside to the south of the backbone ridge was very different. Here were gently rolling hills that provided rich pastureland for cattle, sheep and pigs, with plenty of woodland for timber.

The queen's court at Tamworth came into view, a high-roofed, straw-thatched hall, built on a mound above the river Tame, and surrounded by smaller dwellings. Just one strong palisade protected the settlement, but Egfrid saw shields and spears up on its ramparts. It seemed Queen Cynewise had her own warrior band.

Penda greeted the sight with a huge, joyful bellow. 'Fine food and drink lie ahead,' he cried, 'and a warm welcome from my queen.'

His companions raised a wild din that was answered by horns.

'My daughters will carry spiced mead to us—and

there'll be roasted hog, dripping with fat! What do you say to that?'

Egfrid's stomach clenched with fear. 'Roast hog for you,' he said quietly.

'Roast hog for you too, boy,' Penda said, and slapped him on the shoulder. 'We do not starve our hostages!'

But despite the king's hearty assurance, Egfrid feared what lay ahead.

The great gates of the palisade swung open and they rode into the inner courtyard. The pediment of the hall was carved with ravens, boar's heads and sheaves of corn, painted in vivid shades of crimson and gold. He knew the boars and sheaves were symbols of the goddess Freya, once revered in his homeland Bernicia, but frowned upon now the Bernicians were followers of the Christ-God.

The courtyard thronged with people who pressed forward to greet the returning warriors. One woman strode ahead of the crowd, beautifully dressed in a braid-trimmed gown of red and green. Her faded auburn hair was circled by a golden diadem and garnets gleamed on a chain about her neck.

As she came closer, Egfrid's mouth fell open in shock. This must be Queen Cynewise, and yet he felt sure he'd seen her face before.

Penda climbed down from the saddle and grabbed his wife to steady himself. He covered her face with kisses, while she laughed.

'You stink like a beast,' she told him roundly. 'I'll set the maids to heat water and then we'll see about kissing.'

Egfrid stared, shocked to witness such an open display of affection, and shaken that the queen seemed so familiar. How could he possibly know the wife of his father's greatest enemy?

At last she looked up and saw his pale frightened face. 'And who is this?' she asked.

'This is treasure!' Penda told her. 'Better than gold, he is! This is Faint-heart's son Egfrid, and I've taken him hostage!'

'Oswy's boy?' she murmured. 'A prince of Bernicia? But how...?'

'The fools left him at Bamburgh, there for the taking!'

'You got into the fortress?'

'We had help.' Penda shrugged. 'His nurse tried to dress him in lass's skirts, but we weren't fooled. Perhaps his father will now come out and fight! Better than gold, this boy could be.'

Cynewise looked unsure. 'Oswy is unpredictable,' she warned. 'We'd best take care of his son.'

'Of course' Penda agreed. 'He's a good lad, no harm need come to him! I've brought his holy man and his nurse with him. What more can he want?'

Egfrid, still in the saddle, stared down at the queen, and she chuckled.

'Poor boy, he stares at me as though he's seen a ghost,' she said.

'I think I *have* seen you before, lady,' Egfrid managed.

Penda laughed.

The queen shook her head. 'No, not me,' she said. 'But you must know my younger sister Cyneburgh well.'

Egfrid was more astonished than ever, for he now saw that her face was almost the twin of his aunt's—Oswald Whiteblade's widow.

Cynewise nodded. 'Yes, my sister married the great King Oswald Whiteblade. I see they never told you that her older sister wed the wicked Mercian king?' she added dryly. 'Come here, Oswy's boy, and give me a kiss. You and I are kin by marriage!'

Egfrid slipped down from the saddle to be caught in her arms. Cynewise kissed him warmly, and he saw that his poor widowed aunt was just the pale ghost of her sister.

'Wife, we need food and drink,' Penda cut in. 'First things first. The boy can wait.'

Cynewise turned from Egfrid to laughingly pull her husband's beard. 'Come along, wicked husband,' she said.

CHAPTER 5

Queen's Court

Servants surged after the king and queen and Egfrid was left behind. The connections between their families that the queen had revealed had set his mind racing with dark thoughts. If his aunt was the Mercian queen's sister, then Whiteblade had been Penda's brother-in-law—but Penda had still killed him. Killing kin broke all rules of honour. No wonder there was such bad blood between the two kingdoms.

Egfrid felt a soft touch on his arm and looked round, to find Annis there with Chad. Penda had kept his word and released them.

'What will happen to us now?' he asked.

But before they could answer, the queen returned. Chad bowed courteously and Annis bobbed a curtsey.

Cynewise noted the blackened eye and bruised face. 'We must make you clean and comfortable,' she said. 'I will order a guest house to be prepared. Come with me now.'

They followed her obediently and the queen left them sitting awkwardly for a while at the edge of the hearth, where Penda and his companions had settled to drink and eat. The hall was decorated with brightly painted shields and richly coloured woven tapestries. Servants bustled everywhere with jugs of ale and armfuls of bedding.

Very soon Cynewise returned to take them outside to where a row of neat timber houses stood. The one they were given was furnished with a bed, a truckle, a trestle with stools and a shuttered window-hole that opened onto the courtyard. A fire glowed in the stone hearth and in front of it a tub of warm water steamed. It was both inviting and comfortable, even though two armed warriors stood on guard outside.

A servant brought fresh clothing, but Chad declined it, explaining to the queen that his monk's habit was all he needed, though he'd be glad to shave his head again.

She shook her head amused. 'Well, we will allow you your strange rites, holy man, but tonight we feast to welcome my husband and you must attend—all three of you. I'll leave you to recover from your ride. Send a servant if there's anything you need.'

Despite the queen's kindness and the comfort of their surroundings, as soon they were left alone, Egfrid sat down on the bed, covered his face with his hands and wept.

Annis sat down beside him and tried to hug him, but he turned away from her. 'Don't,' he ordered.

Chad understood. 'Leave him,' he said, gently. 'He has a right to weep.'

Annis went reluctantly to examine the clothing the servants had brought, while Egfrid struggled to regain his dignity.

At last he dashed his tears away and raised his head. 'What will they do to me now?' he asked. 'I'm captured by the man who killed my uncle. I'm disgraced and my father will be furious.'

Chad sat down beside him. 'He should not be furious with you,' he said.

'But what will they *do* with me?'

'I don't know,' Chad admitted. 'But now they have us safe in Mercia, they seem to treat us kindly.'

Annis lifted a tunic. 'These clothes are good,' she said.

'This is twice madder dyed, trimmed with tablet weave and just a little worn. And the gowns they've brought for me are far too good.'

Both boy and monk smiled at the cheerful note that had crept into her voice.

'I'm glad you are both here with me,' Egfrid admitted.

'Clothing and comfortable accommodation must mean they'll let us live,' Chad said. 'I think they might demand a ransom from your father.'

Egfrid shuddered. 'He will be furious if he is forced to give the Mercians gold.'

'They might want land,' Chad suggested.

'He'd hate that even more!'

'Well,' said Chad, 'we are here and must make the best of it. We are alive and together, praise God.'

'Praise God,' Annis echoed with feeling.

'Amen,' Egfrid added.

'I shall sit outside and leave you for a while to wash and dress,' Chad said.

As the monk went, Annis gently started to peel Egfrid's dirty tunic away from his bruised shoulders.

Chad appeared again, as the light began to fade. He'd brushed his habit and shaved the stubble from his chin and forehead. 'We're to go to the feasting hall,' he said.

Annis too had washed and dressed in the gown she thought so fine. Apart from their bruises, they looked more their usual selves again.

Warm smells of food drifted from the huts all around the feasting hall. The guards fell in behind them as they left the shelter of their guest hut. Penda's great meeting place was as large as any Oswy Iding owned, but noisier and more crowded than the hall at Bamburgh. They hovered uncertainly on the threshold.

'Where should we go?' Egfrid asked uncertainly.

Penda and Cynewise were seated at a trestle, on a raised dais, close to the fire. Hunting dogs and a few cats lazed around the long hearth. Warriors and richly gowned women filled the hall with a great deal of noise and cheerful greeting. Queen Cynewise saw them hesitating and beckoned them inside.

'Come, join us at the high table. Yes, you too, the nurse and the holy man. Sit there opposite Woden's priest. No Christian wizardry here!' she added with quiet amusement.

Chad was placed across the table from a gnarled old man in a horned headdress. Annis nervously took her place, unused to being treated as a guest.

A horn sounded three blasts and to the sound of

drums, a procession of richly dressed young women entered the hall, carrying heavy, gold-trimmed mead-horns. Cynewise took the largest one and offered it to Penda.

'I've been looking forward to this,' the king announced. He tipped the horn and took a long pull at the sweet drink. Everyone cheered as he finished with a huge burp. The feast had begun.

Musicians strummed lutes as food was carried in from the kitchen huts outside and delicious scents drifted across the hall. As Penda had promised, a crisp boar's head that steamed and crackled was presented on a silver charger.

Penda hacked at it with his knife. 'Here, give this to the boy,' he said, handing a generous portion to his wife to pass on to Egfrid. 'He will never have tasted anything so good. I promised him this as we rode through the night.'

Everyone turned to watch as Egfrid lifted the golden delicacy to his lips and began to crunch on it. There were low chuckles at the look of pleasure that came unbidden to his face.

Sheep's haunches cooked in herbs and wine appeared, along with roasted swan and goose, served with rich buttery sauces and soft white bread. Egfrid realised he was hungry, but looked up in alarm at Annis. 'Could it be poisoned?' he whispered.

She turned at once to Chad, her own hand hovering halfway to her mouth.

Chad gave a small shake of his head and calmly took a bite from a hunk of bread. They ate and couldn't help but enjoy the food. A sharp tug on his tunic made Egfrid glance beneath the table, to find a small mottled hound boldly pawing his knee. He kicked it away, longing miserably for his own dog Woodruff.

CHAPTER 6

Queen's Boon

The hall was filled with the sound of loud voices and the clatter of gold and silver plates, as one delicious dish after another was presented.

When a lull made it possible to speak, the queen turned to Egfrid. 'The princess who led the procession is my oldest daughter Cyneburgh,' she told him. 'She's named for my sister and all our young warriors want to marry her.'

Egfrid nodded politely.

The queen's expression changed. 'Tell me, how is my sister, the widowed queen?'

Egfrid shrugged. 'She wants to be a nun,' he said.

Cynewise looked thoughtful. 'I remember a pale, quiet girl. We never saw each other again once I'd married Penda. My father converted to the Christian faith, but I had come to Mercia as a peace-weaver bride and felt that I couldn't betray the gods of my husband's kingdom. Your holy man might disagree, I think.'

Egfrid made no reply. He sensed that the queen was not really talking to him, but to Chad.

Woden's priest turned angrily to the Christian monk, expecting a response that he could challenge, but Chad refused to rise to the provocation.

'You are a loyal wife, lady,' he said.

The queen smiled. 'And I see that you are something of a peace-maker too. That is my son,' she said, pointing to a young man with a pleasant face who sat at the king's right hand. 'His father always called him Beorn—little bear—and now he's known as Prince Beorn.'

Beorn raised his drink-horn to them in a cheerful manner. 'Drink-hail!' he cried.

Egfrid could not help but smile.

'Beorn is soon to be made king of the Middle Angles,' Cynewise added proudly.

'I think you have a younger son, lady,' Egfrid said. 'One who trains to be a warrior?'

'Yes,' she said wistfully. 'Wulfhere lives with his foster-father, one of Mercia's greatest warriors. He'll come back to us soon when he is battle-trained.'

Egfrid sensed that he'd saddened her, but that made him resentful, for he had a mother who must be terrified for him.

'My mother will weep when she knows I'm taken hostage,' he said.

Cynewise nodded. 'Yes, she'll weep,' she agreed. 'Any mother would weep.'

The queen sat quietly for a while and then turned from Egfrid to talk to her husband. The soft damp nose of the young hound came pushing into the boy's hand for food again and with a sigh, he took a titbit from the table and fed it.

The feast rolled on, as jugglers performed in the space behind the fire. Acrobats walked on their hands and danced to the rhythm of drums, followed by a girl with trained dogs that jumped through hoops and twisted through her legs. This act caused something of a commotion, for the creatures' antics set the hunting hounds baying.

At last the girl, her dogs and the hunting hounds were all shooed out of the hall, growling and snatching meat bones as they passed. Egfrid looked for the friendly pup, but he seemed to have gone with the rest.

The hall grew quieter when they'd gone, and Penda

sat back in his carved wooden chair and stroked his beard. He looked thoughtfully across at Egfrid, and then suddenly called forward the warriors who'd ridden north with him. They received gifts, gold armbands, rings and brooches—rewards for their loyalty and support.

'Shall we summon the songsters and fetch the harp-stool?' Beorn asked when the gift-giving came to an end.

'Not yet,' Penda said. 'I have something important to say. One more gift to bestow.'

Beorn looked somewhat surprised, but he stood up at once and beat the hilt of his meat knife loudly on a bronze platter to call for silence. All faces turned to the king.

'My dear wife Cynewise has begged a boon of me,' Penda announced. 'And I am minded to grant her wish, for no king could have a more wise and loyal queen.' He turned towards Egfrid and said, 'Step forward, Oswy's boy!'

The feasters turned to stare and Egfrid's stomach lurched. He wished he hadn't eaten quite so much for suddenly he felt sick. Chad put a protective hand on Egfrid's shoulder.

'You too, holy man,' the king said, seeing the gesture. 'And bring the little nurse-maid too!'

Annis paled, but she bravely got up and led the way around the table, so that all three of them stood at the front of the dais.

Penda and Cynewise both rose from their seats, the queen taking the king's arm to help him.

'Stand by me, boy,' the king said.

Egfrid glanced nervously for a hidden weapon, but the old warrior's gnarled palm appeared empty. Feeling there was no choice, he obediently went to stand by the king.

'I ask you, holy man of Bernicia, and my companions to bear witness to what I now do,' Penda said.

Egfrid feared that his throat might be cut, but instead he found that Penda laid a hand gently on his head and spoke the most astonishing words. 'I, Penda, King of Mercia do take Egfrid, Prince of Bernicia to be my foster-son.'

There came an audible gasp from all who watched. Egfrid blinked, thinking this must be some foolish dream.

'I will treat this boy as I would my own son,' the king finished, formally. 'By Woden, I do swear it!'

Annis and Chad glanced at each other and then stared back at the king in amazement.

'Do you, holy man, bear witness to this honourable oath?' Penda asked.

'I do,' Chad said quickly.

There was another moment of stunned silence, and then cheering broke out. Egfrid caught the eye of the woman Fritha, who sat near the fire looking clean and tidy. She nodded secretively and smiled.

The feasters hammered their knives on the wooden trestles, for it seemed the king's generous gesture had met with their approval.

Cynewise kissed Egfrid on both cheeks. 'Now we are kin by foster vows,' she said. 'And I am your foster-mother.'

'Thank you,' Egfrid whispered, for he knew that she was to thank for this. No great king could ever kill his foster-son.

'Tell the bard to sing of what he's witnessed,' Penda ordered.

Everyone sat down and Egfrid returned to his seat, feeling dazed. Had this really happened and what did it mean? Was he still a hostage?

The bard came forward, searching quickly to find words to praise this unexpected turn of events. After a moment he struck the strings of his harp and looked up with a confident smile.

'A young eagle flew from his eyrie,
Seeking a famous foster-father
A stout-hearted hero
To teach him the way of the warrior
And take him under his wing.
How could such a man be found?
A wide-ruler, a warrior of worth
Fearless in fighting; the bane of his foes,
Only the powerful, praise-worthy Penda
Could answer the young eagle's call!'

Everyone smiled, impressed by the bard's skilful quick thinking. One songster followed another, with wilder praise, though Penda appeared exhausted. Cynewise leant forward to gently take the drink-horn from her husband's hand.

'Holy man,' she said, turning to Chad. 'Take my foster son and his nursemaid back to your hut. He has a hard day's work ahead of him tomorrow.'

'Am I still a hostage?' Egfrid asked wearily, as they stumbled across the courtyard. The two guards followed and took up their position once again.

'I fear so,' Chad said quietly. 'We will talk again in the morning.'

'Where will *you* sleep?' Annis asked him.

'I shall lie across the threshold,' he said. 'I am used to hard floors.'

She nodded. 'I'm glad of that,' she said.

And Egfrid knew that, king's foster-son or not, they must never drop their guard.

CHAPTER 7

Another Familiar Face

Next morning Egfrid woke wondering whether he'd had a strange dream. Chad and Annis were eating breakfast by the hearth. He sat up in bed. 'Am I the king and queen's foster-son?' he asked them uncertainly.

They smiled at each other.

'The king swore by his god Woden,' said Chad. 'I don't think Penda's a man to break his oath.'

'But…if I am his foster-child and to be treated as his son, then am I not free to go home if I wish?'

'I think not,' said Chad. 'A foster-son cannot go running home whenever he wishes. Wulfhere cannot come back to his mother until he is warrior-trained.'

'But, it must be a good thing,' Annis hastened to say. 'For surely it means that no harm can come to you. Now eat some of this porridge I've kept warm for you.'

No sooner was Egfrid dressed and breakfasted than the queen sent a servant to escort him and Chad to the stables, where they found her waiting.

'Do you ride?' she asked.

'Yes,' Egfrid said, uncertainly.

A groom led forward a sturdy bay gelding with a sand-coloured mane and tail. The horse was fitted with a soft leather saddle and bridle.

'He's yours,' said the queen.

Egfrid couldn't stop smiling. The gelding was a handsome beast, though taller than any mount he'd ridden. Perhaps Annis was right: there was much to be gained from being treated as a foster child. 'What is he called?' he asked.

'Golden-mane. Can you get up into the saddle?'

Egfrid nodded eagerly and Chad bent to help him mount as Cynewise watched with approval.

'We will ride out,' she said.

'Lady, I must keep the boy in my sight,' Chad told her.

'I hope you can ride fast, holy man,' she said.

She mounted a silver-grey mare with the ease of an experienced horsewoman, while a nervous roan was led forward for Chad. Cynewise headed out through the main gate towards a stretch of rolling grassland, urging her mare to canter. Egfrid clung on tightly and tried to keep up, while Chad just managed to stay in sight.

They returned to Tamworth when the sun was high, and after a brief meal in the queen's great hall, Penda called Egfrid to him.

'Now we will turn you into a warrior,' he said. 'Follow me!'

Egfrid, still a little breathless from his fast ride, dared not complain. Penda led the way to the training ground, where a muscular man was waiting for them.

'Sigurd is your battle-master,' Penda said. 'He is captain of the queen's warrior band. Start with the spear, Sigurd, just as with my own sons. Then, when he has mastered that, we shall see about lifting a sword.'

Egfrid's mind swung into confusion with more of the troubling thoughts that had come to him on the journey. If he learned warrior skills, then surely his first duty as his father's son must be to kill the Mercian king? But how would the Christ-God regard one who killed his foster-father?

The king left them. Egfrid saw that he limped badly as he walked away; Penda could not fight for ever.

'Come forward,' Sigurd ordered.

Egfrid summoned his courage, lifted his chin and stepped forward. Soon there was no time to worry or fret for the Mercian was a strict taskmaster. Chad watched anxiously, never taking his eyes from his charge as he struggled to copy lunging movements with a light spear and shield.

As the light began to fade, Sigurd told him to put what he'd learned into practice. 'Come at me boy,' he said. 'Attack is the best defence! Come at me as though you mean to kill me!'

Egfrid hesitated. 'Come at me,' Sigurd growled. 'Or are you a cowardly faint-heart like your father?'

Anger rose. Egfrid thought of the dark bruise still there on Annis's face, and he lunged at his battle-master shouting curses, only to find that Sigurd skilfully turned the weapon aside, using his shield.

'Aah!' Egfrid groaned.

Sigurd grinned. 'Enough for one day! We will make a warrior out of you yet!'

Egfrid felt battered from head to toe, but also strangely elated.

Back in his chamber Annis fretted over his hurts, gently applying marigold balm. 'I didn't refuse, or complain,' he told her with fierce pride.

'No,' Chad, agreed. 'He didn't.'

Just before the evening meal, they heard horns and shouting, followed by the sound of hooves. All three looked up at each other, anxious as to what this might mean.

'I'll see what it is,' Chad said.

He returned quickly, his expression bright. 'Better news, I think. Prince Ethelwald has arrived. Your father has sent your cousin to act as a go-between. He's come to ask for your safe return.'

'My cousin Ethelwald—Whiteblade's son? Can I go home then?' Egfrid asked. His father had not abandoned him to his fate as he feared he might.

Chad shook his head. 'Don't get your hopes up. Coming to an agreement could take a long time, but it is a start.'

'How long?' Egfrid asked uneasily.

'It could take months or years.'

Egfrid answered sulkily, 'You call that better news?'

'Yes,' Chad insisted. 'Now you may go to the feast-hall and I'd advise you to speak to your cousin politely.'

The trestles were laid for the evening meal and Ethelwald lolled in a chair beside the fire, a horn of mead in his hand. He and Beorn chatted like old friends, while Penda and Cynewise watched them with smiling tolerance. A pretty servant girl stroked Ethelwald's hair and repeatedly kissed him.

Egfrid realised with a jolt that his cousin must be a regular visitor here.

Ethelwald turned and saw him. 'Come, kiss me, cousin and be cheerful,' he said. 'Your lady mother is distraught at your loss. And your father is angry,' he added with a hint of a smile.

Egfrid kissed him, coolly. Perhaps he didn't know his handsome cousin as well as he wished—and did his father realise quite how familiar Ethelwald was at the Mercian court?

'Do the wicked pagans treat you well?' Ethelwald asked, slipping a quick sideways smile towards Cynewise.

'Yes,' Egfrid said, lifting his chin a little. 'The king has made me his foster-son.'

'He what?' Ethelwald sat bolt upright, his jaw dropping.

Penda chuckled. 'And worth it just to see your face,' he said.

'Foster-son?' Ethelwald gasped. 'But where does that leave my negotiations? I thought you'd want land or gold, or both.'

Penda leaned back in his chair and stroked his beard. 'My queen had much to do with it,' he admitted. 'Maybe I grow soft with age and weary of harrying a man who only knows how to retreat. Cynewise longs to see your mother and she's persuaded me that the time has come for a peace agreement.'

'Could I go home then?' Egfrid asked.

The adults glanced at each other.

'No, boy,' Penda said firmly. 'Ethelwald will report that we take good care of you and tell Oswy he has till Blood-month to consider a peace agreement.'

'Peace between Bernicia and Mercia?' Ethelwald said. 'Such a thing I never thought to see.'

'I want to see my sister,' Cynewise told her nephew. 'And I want an end to this blood-feud. We suggest an exchange of gifts, and Oswy's oldest daughter as a peace-weaver bride for Beorn. Let us seal our agreement with kinship.'

Beorn winked at Egfrid. 'I hear Princess Alchfled is very beautiful,' he said.

Ethelwald laughed. 'Alchfled and you? Chalk and cheese!' he said. 'But she'd make another hostage, should things not work out well. What do *you* say, Egfrid?'

Egfrid said nothing, for he felt Chad's warning pressure on his shoulder. His oldest sister Alchfled was beautiful in a delicate, willowy way, but she was a devout Christian and he could not imagine her here in this hall, with images of Woden and Freya everywhere. Had the world gone mad?

Silence followed, while they all considered this unlikely match.

'We'll eat now,' Penda said, and got up to move to the table.

Ethelwald whispered in Egfrid's ear, 'How did you tame the old battle-bruiser?'

Egfrid shrugged, for he was just as surprised as his cousin.

They watched as Penda stumped to the table and awkwardly eased himself into his seat.

'His wound pains him,' Egfrid said. 'Perhaps he's had enough of fighting.'

'He's not the man he was,' Ethelwald agreed. 'But I can't see the old bear dying in his bed. He's simply found a clever new way of making Oswy squirm.'

They took their places at table and the food was just as lavish as the night before. Egfrid filled his belly, never thinking once of poison. The hound came again and he fed it choice titbits, but once his hunger was satisfied, his eyelids started to droop.

'Take my foster-son to his bed,' Cynewise instructed Chad. 'He's had a long, hard day of it.'

Annis helped Egfrid undress, but as he lay down to sleep, a troubling thought came. Those traitors who'd opened the gates of Bamburgh had once been Ethelwald's men. They'd got what they deserved, but... had his cousin known what they were about? Could he trust Ethelwald, any more than he could trust the Mercians?

CHAPTER 8
The World Turned Upside Down

Next morning, Egfrid and Chad were called early to attend the king and queen. They found them with Beorn and Ethelwald.

'Your cousin is setting off to York with gifts for your parents and for Princess Alchfled,' Cynewise told him.

Egfrid bowed. 'My sister will be honoured,' he said tactfully.

Cynewise hesitated before her next announcement, as though she knew it might bring sorrow. 'Your nurse must go back with him,' she said. 'It is a gesture of good will, and she will bear witness that we treat you kindly.'

Egfrid was shocked.

Chad quickly intervened, making it clear that he

would be staying. 'I can serve the prince, in every way that's needed,' he said.

'The time is done for having a nursemaid,' Penda said gruffly. 'My foster-son needs no nurse to coddle him. Is that not right?'

Egfrid swallowed hard. 'Yes, sir,' he managed.

But as soon as they were back in the guest hut, his courage failed and he rushed headlong into Annis's arms. 'You are to go back,' he cried. 'They are saying you must go, and leave me here.'

Annis looked up, alarmed, as Chad quietly followed him into the room.

'I cannot leave my boy,' she cried.

'But I think you must,' Chad said. 'If you return, you can reassure Queen Eanfleda that our prince is safe and well. It's a gesture of good faith on the Mercians' part and we must accept it.'

'But who will see to his clothes and his hurts?' Annis looked distraught.

'I will,' Chad said. 'I have healing skills and I can wash and dry clothes and smooth them with slick stones.'

'But such work…it is too humble for a holy man.'

Chad smiled. 'I'm the youngest of five brothers,'

he said. 'Do you think I've never played the servant before? My duty as the prince's tutor now means more than teaching him to read and write. Besides,' he added, 'nothing is too humble for a Christian holy man.'

'I know you'd give your life to protect him,' Annis admitted sadly.

'Do you want to go home?' Egfrid asked.

Her brief hesitation told him that she did. 'I... I don't want to leave you,' she began, 'but my mother is old and sick, she may not last the winter and...' She halted.

Egfrid glanced at Chad, and took a deep breath. 'You must go,' he said. 'I can manage here, so long as Chad is with me.'

Annis looked as though she might cry, but instead she hugged him. 'I'll come back if you send for me,' she whispered, her voice breaking with emotion. 'And I will always be your loving Annis.'

'I know you will,' Egfrid said. He smiled bravely now, for a happier thought had followed. 'Please, will you search for Woodruff, and if you find him, see that he is well fed and treated kindly.'

'I'll take him to my home and keep him myself,' she said.

Ethelwald rode away from Tamworth with a wagonload of gifts and a contingent of armed Mercians to guard it, in addition to his own warrior band. Annis was provided with a steady cob and allowed to take the new clothes with her. The queen added a small gold brooch in the shape of a dragon, with a garnet in its eye, for she said that the nurse had behaved with a dragon's courage.

Egfrid and Chad stood on the palisade walkway, above the main gate, and watched as the cavalcade vanished into the distance. As they turned away, Sigurd strode out from the training ground, the spotted hound on a leash beside him.

'Time for another bout of spear-work, lad,' he said. 'Before the sun sets and the meal is ready.'

Egfrid reached forward to fondle the hound's silky ears as it reared to lick his hand.

'And Queen Cynewise says you're to have this beast and keep him with you for protection, if you wish it.'

'I wish it,' Egfrid said quickly, his spirits lifting. 'What is his name?'

'You may name him as you like.'

'Dapple,' the boy said, 'for he's dappled like a deer.'

'Then Dapple he is. Give him to your holy man, while we work on your stance and feet.'

Chad took the dog and followed them to the training ground. Dapple trotted obediently in his new master's wake.

The following days fell into a hard pattern of work. Egfrid rose at dawn each day to work with shield and spear, and sometimes wrestled with Sigurd's son, Ranulf. The first time he managed to throw the bigger lad, he whooped wildly with delight, and then hurried to help him up.

'You won't do that again, in a hurry,' Ranulf said cheerfully, dusting himself down.

Dapple went everywhere at his master's heels and slept at the bottom of Egfrid's bed. He brought comfort whenever the boy's thoughts strayed to the loss of Annis, and woke with a growl when the slightest sound or movement disturbed their sleep.

As Weed-month began, the weather grew warm. Chad, concerned that Egfrid might forget his book-learning, spoke to the queen. 'Christian princes are expected to learn such skills,' he told her.

'But I'm training to be a warrior now,' Egfrid protested, uncertain that he wanted to return to books.

'Ethelwald can read and write,' Cynewise acknowledged. 'But my husband scorns such skills... not the way of the warrior king.'

'Writing can be put to good use,' Chad persisted. 'Your sister, the widowed queen, reads well. I could write a letter to her from you.'

The queen looked up with interest. 'Very well,' she said. 'Write a message to my sister for me, and my foster son shall have his lessons again.'

Chad searched for goose quills, dipped the tips in boiling water and sharpened them to make pens. He made ink by crushing the round galls from oak trees. The queen bought vellum from a travelling merchant and a private message was written and sent to the widowed Queen Cyneburgh.

Though Penda struggled more than ever with his painful leg, he often stumped outside to watch Egfrid's training sessions and give advice and praise.

The weather turned cool as Offerings-month began, and still no word came from King Oswy. Egfrid knew his father would hate to make peace with such a bitter enemy, but as the Night of the Dead approached, Ethelwald arrived back in Tamworth.

He too brought a wagonload of gifts and the news

that Oswy waited at Londesbrough, on the north bank of the Humber, where—with the King of Deira's permission—a meeting could take place.

'They agree to Princess Alchfled as a peace-weaver bride for Beorn,' Ethelwald announced. 'But they want more.'

'What more?' Penda demanded.

Ethelwald grinned as Cynewise's golden-haired eldest daughter presented him with a gold-rimmed drink-horn of mead. 'They want your Cyneburgh for Oswy's eldest son.'

'Huh!' Penda growled. 'Can he run as fast as his father then?'

Ethelwald snorted with laughter.

The queen was all smiles at the suggestion, though the young princess looked somewhat unsure.

'They propose a meeting and an exchange of brides at Londesbrough. Oswin the Good is willing to act as host and it can be done before Blood-month begins.'

'Oh, husband,' Cynewise touched Penda's arm, imploring his consent.

The king moved his leg and groaned. 'Very well,' he growled. 'I cannot lead an army like this. It seems we must make peace with Faint-heart.'

Cynewise flung her arms about him and drink-horns were raised to the coming peace agreement.

CHAPTER 9

Peace

Egfrid's spirits swung wildly back and forth as he rode through the backbone hills, heading towards the flat wet-lands that surrounded the Humber. They made slow progress, due to Penda's wound, which gave him more pain than ever. Sometimes Egfrid fizzed with excitement— he'd see his parents again! At other times his thoughts drifted back to the earlier journey, when he'd ridden in front of Penda, fearful that he'd be killed at any moment.

Chad saw the way his thoughts strayed. 'A better journey,' he said.

'Better for you,' Egfrid, answered, remembering the black eye the monk had suffered. 'But not better for the king!' he added, with a backward glance to where Penda was carried in a wagon.

'No indeed,' Chad agreed.

Penda had refused to be left in Tamworth like an old mule put out to grass, but he suffered the indignity of the wagon with impatience. Cynewise rode at his side, patiently doing all she could to ease his pain. Fritha tended the king each time they made camp.

They forded the River Humber at the ancient crossing place, close to the remains of the old Roman camp at Brough. After one night's rest, they moved on to Londesburgh and when they came in sight of the palisade, they found it surrounded by a great spread of tents, all marked by different battle standards.

Egfrid's stomach churned at the sight. What would it be like to meet his parents again, in front of this vast gathering? He knew he couldn't return to Bamburgh and wondered how it would feel to say goodbye again.

Horns blared to announce their arrival and Oswy and his queen rode out to meet them. Egfrid sat tall in the saddle, glad that Cynewise had insisted that he wear his new leather warrior's jacket and a soft woollen cloak dyed in rich purple. What would his father think when he saw him dressed as royally as his cousin Ethelwald?

Horns blared again as the two parties lifted their hands in greeting. Oswy swung down from the saddle and strode past Egfrid to Penda, who was carried uncomfortably upright on his carved gold-painted throne.

Egfrid was dismayed that his father did not even appear to have noticed him. But his mother had seen him. Eanfleda rushed towards him, tears pouring down her cheeks.

'My son, my son!' she cried. Egfrid found himself enveloped in a loving, though rather damp embrace— at least somebody had missed him.

'It's all right, Mother,' he whispered. 'I'm safe.'

'Dear boy, dear boy,' she cried. 'Have they made you take part in their wicked pagan ceremonies?'

'No, Mother. Chad is always at my side. I am allowed my faith.'

'King Oswy Iding welcomes the great King Penda to Deira,' a herald announced.

Penda's throne was lowered to the ground and he struggled painfully to his feet. 'Oswin Yffi should be the one to welcome us,' he said.

Young King Oswin hurried forward, eager to make amends.

Penda gripped the younger man's hand warmly and only then turned to Oswy, nodding curtly. Cynewise hurried to her husband's side, anxious to smooth things over.

The herald announced, 'Queen Cyneburgh, widow of the late and great King Oswald Whiteblade.'

A curtained litter was carried forwards and Cynewise took a few nervous steps towards it, her expression strained. The curtains opened and Whiteblade's widow stepped out to greet the older sister she hadn't seen since she was a child. Everyone gasped as the two women, so alike and yet so different, kissed, then hugged each other tightly.

Cynewise gave a fierce smile 'I named my first daughter in your honour,' she said.

The tension that had surrounded the men lifted a little and there followed a light ripple of applause. What further was said between the two sisters could not be heard, but Cynewise led her sister to Penda, and the old man bowed over the widowed queen's hand and kissed it.

'Your husband was a true warrior, lady,' he said. 'I regret his death.'

Cyneburgh lifted her chin a little. 'I am a Christian. I forgive,' she said.

'You forgive your husband's killer?' Penda said, surprised.

'I do,' she said firmly.

Penda bowed to her again.

Egfrid suddenly saw his poor aunt in a new, courageous light.

There was another awkward pause and then Oswy led Alchfled forward. 'My daughter the peace-weaver bride,' he announced.

Even Egfrid was impressed, Alchfled had never looked so fine, her long fair hair brushed loose and falling about her shoulders. She was dressed in red trimmed with gold braiding, and carried a mead-horn that she proffered to the grizzled old Mercian. He took a sip and handed it back to her, then landed a smacking kiss on her cheek that startled her.

'My daughter is also a peace-weaver bride, named after her aunt,' he said, and the younger Cyneburgh emerged from amongst her waiting women, also beautifully dressed and escorted by an eager, smiling Prince Beorn.

Both couples who were to marry bowed and curtsied to each other, then dutifully kissed. Egfrid was glad he wasn't old enough to be ordered to marry an enemy bride for the sake of peace. What must they really be feeling?

More drinks were proffered and accepted and Oswin the Good invited them to a feast.

'Should not Oswy Iding greet my foster-son first?' Penda asked.

Oswy turned pale and glanced about him, clearly discomforted. Egfrid's mother led him forward to his father, who quickly recovered and kissed him on both cheeks.

'You've grown,' he said. 'I…almost didn't know you.'

Egfrid bowed. 'I am well, Father,' he said curtly.

'We are training him in courage,' Penda said pointedly.

Anger blazed for a moment in Oswy's blue eyes but was swiftly suppressed. 'Come, the feast is prepared,' was all he said.

Egfrid saw that every word that passed between those two had a deeper, darker meaning, but everyone moved politely off towards the main gateway. Great show was made of setting weapons aside in the sheltered porch as they entered the hall, while slaves and servants started to raise the tents. They made a Mercian camp well away from the Bernician one—and left a wide swathe of no-man's land between them.

The feast Oswin the Good provided was lavish and the talk cordial, but as the mead was passed and the night wore on, spirits grew reckless. Egfrid recognised the low-voiced singing of a Bernician battle song, and whispered riddles that contained hidden insults. The earlier goodwill began to turn sour.

Queen Eanfleda went to join Cynewise and her sister, who'd been sitting together, their heads bowed in close conversation. The three queens rose as one and a sudden hush fell over the hall.

'We thank our dear cousin Oswin for providing such an excellent feast,' Eanfleda began, 'but we have much to discuss in the morning.'

The three women faced their men with determination. 'True peace between our kingdoms must depend on clear heads,' said Cynewise. 'It is time for us all to go to our beds.'

Penda chuckled and nodded at Oswy. 'I think we are dismissed,' he said.

They got up and left the hall for the comfort of their beds.

CHAPTER 10
A Battle of Words

Formal negotiations took place in the morning, and Egfrid and Chad attended the meeting of the kings. The two bitter enemies Penda and Oswy faced each other on their thrones, their queens at their side on smaller seats.

A snag rose in the smooth running of the agreement, for Oswy insisted that Prince Beorn should become a Christian, if he was to wed the devout Princess Alchfled.

Penda's face turned red with rage. The Mercian priest of Woden raised his raven wand and began to mutter curses, but Beorn spoke quietly to his father and after a few tense moments Chad was called to join them.

Beorn then made an announcement. 'My father agrees that I should speak for myself in this,' he said.

'I am willing to take instruction in the Christian religion, and Brother Chad, Prince Egfrid's tutor, is willing to teach me. Then, if I truly come to believe that the Christ-God's way is a better way I shall become a Christian. My father agrees that I should choose such a thing of my own free will.'

This speech was followed by nods of approval from both sides. Young Princess Cyneburgh spoke quietly to her father, and Penda kissed her. 'My daughter will take Christian instruction too,' he said. 'She will make her own choice. I do not force my children one way or another. Are you content with that?'

Cynewise flashed him a look of gratitude.

Oswy said, 'I am content.'

Somehow Penda had scored a point, whilst appearing to give ground, and Egfrid sensed that his father raged in silence.

'This is a battle fought with words,' he said quietly to Chad.

The monk nodded grimly. 'Better than a battle of swords,' he said. 'No life is lost—no blood is shed.'

The weddings took place that afternoon. Lavish gifts of gold and jewels were exchanged and suddenly it was almost over. The final feast was ready and preparations were made to return to Tamworth—the only difference being that pretty young Cyneburgh would ride away to Bamburgh, while Alchfled would be riding in the Mercian train with him.

Egfrid had just dressed for the feast when Cynewise called him to her tent. 'Penda has given permission for you to see your parents,' she said. 'Chad will escort you to King Oswy's chamber.'

Egfrid smiled. 'Thank you, lady,' he said. 'This is your doing, I think.'

'Remember you are still my foster-son,' she said.

Egfrid's mother welcomed him with more kisses, while his father sat in his chair looking uncomfortable. Chad hovered in the doorway, to allow them privacy.

'My poor son,' his mother said. 'Your courage has brought about this peace. Do you suffer very much, being forced to live with wicked pagans?'

'They treat me kindly,' Egfrid said. 'I have my own gelding and hound.' He wished his father would speak, rather than watch him darkly from the other side of the room.

At last Oswy looked up.

'Never trust them,' he said. 'This peace may not hold, for I will never believe the word of any Mercian, and neither Oswin the Perfect nor Ethelwald are all they seem to be.'

Egfrid nodded, knowing that his father was right to doubt their loyalty.

'Londesbrough should be mine,' Oswy said, as he glanced around him at the strongly built oak beams and rich wall hangings. 'My brother ruled both Deira and Bernicia. Your mother is the daughter of Edwin of Deira. I have a better right to rule here than the Perfect One ever had.'

Eanfleda sighed. 'But surely this chance for peace must make it worth giving a little,' she said.

'We give too much,' Oswy said sharply. Then he seemed to recollect his son's vulnerable position. 'Keep Chad at your side,' he said. 'For there at least is one you can trust. Your mother has brought vellum and ink to help you in your lessons.'

Egfrid sighed. He wished they'd brought Woodruff instead, but he thanked them politely as Chad gathered up the vellum rolls and sealed inkhorns, and put them carefully into his leather scrip.

The sounding of horns announced the final meal.

Eanfleda kissed her son again and Egfrid's brief moment with his parents was over. They made their way to the great hall and took their places for the last feast.

The following morning, Alchfled was given a box of jewels and a gift of land from Prince Beorn, as her morning-gift. This finalised the wedding ceremony and made them husband and wife, for good or ill. The bride blushed and smiled in a way that surprised Egfrid. Perhaps it would not be so bad a thing to have his sister with him at the Mercian court.

Queen Eanfleda came to him as the Mercians mounted up to leave. 'Dear boy, stay strong and pray to the Christ-God that you will soon be released. I pray for it every day.'

'I will be strong, Mother,' he agreed.

Then she dropped her voice and whispered, 'Don't fret that your father doesn't come to say farewell. He cannot bear to let them see that he suffers by your exile…and he does suffer greatly. He is deeply humiliated to see you as Penda's foster-son.'

Egfrid swallowed hard. 'But I am not humiliated by it. Queen Cynewise is my friend.'

'Yes.' Eanfleda nodded. 'She is a good woman, almost as good as her sister. If only she knew the true faith then she would be truly good.'

This mild criticism of the Mercian queen rankled. Egfrid kissed his mother and swung himself up onto Golden-mane's back, feeling strangely eager to ride away.

The journey-mead was drunk, horns blared, and the Mercian cavalcade moved off. Egfrid saw tears on his sister's cheek and urged his horse forward to ride at her side.

'Don't fear, sister,' he said. 'I have much to show you at Tamworth.'

'Dear, brave little brother,' she said. 'You will be a comfort to me. Will you come to pray with me in Mercia? I mean to build a Christian church on the land that Beorn has given me—will you help with my plans?'

Egfrid smiled reassuringly at her, but when she fell silent he allowed his horse to drop back to ride beside Chad and Fritha.

'I tried to cheer my sister,' he told the monk. 'But I think you could bring her more comfort than me.'

Chad urged his mare forward, while Egfrid fell in with Fritha.

'How is that hound of yours doing?' she asked.

Egfrid smiled. 'He comes whenever I call.'

They reached Tamworth just in time for the Night of the Dead, the feast that the Christians called All Hallows Eve. Alchfled refused to take part in the pagan celebration and suggested that Egfrid come to her small private hall to pray. Aware of the disappointment on the boy's face, Beorn offered to stay with his bride instead.

'I wish I could see the Night of the Dead,' Egfrid told Chad, once they were out of his sister's hearing. 'Fritha says there will be dancing after dark and fires lit on the hillside. I would not worship the death-goddess. I would only watch to see what happens.'

Chad thought for a moment. 'I'll come with you,' he said. 'We may both learn something. To know about such things is part of your education, I think.'

Egfrid grinned. 'I'll be safe with you and Dapple,' he said.

The Mercians baked cakes and carried them to the shrine of Hella, the death-goddess. Though the food and drink were meant for the dead, they seemed to be eaten by the living, and once darkness fell wild music and dancing began. The boy and the monk sat on the shadowy hillside with Dapple at their side and watched, faint smiles upon their faces.

Blood-month followed and just as in Bernicia, the cattle were slaughtered and butchered, their carcases salted or smoked. Only the breeding cows were saved for spring. Every hut and dwelling had joints and haunches hanging above the fires. The weather grew cold and Yule was celebrated with more fires, feast and drinking. The guards no longer stood outside Egfrid's guest house.

CHAPTER 11

A Coward's Act

All through the winter Egfrid trained, and no amount of ice or snow provided an excuse. His determination to succeed was strengthened whenever Penda rewarded him with a nod or grunt of approval. As the days lengthened, an exhilarating new sensation of bodily strength came to the boy. His spear flew further and hit its mark more often. The muscles in his body grew hard, so that swinging an axe and lifting a shield became easier. On rare, wonderful occasions he managed to knock Ranulf down, and once he caught Sigurd off-guard and landed a well-aimed blow. His teacher got up, looking startled, while Ranulf laughed.

In the early days his sister called him to her chamber

and made him kneel to pray, but those times grew rarer. More often than not, it was Chad who went to pray with both Beorn and his bride. The Mercian prince took his promise to study Christianity seriously.

Penda watched his son with brooding concern, and sometimes tempered his newfound enthusiasm for the Christ-God with a few sharp warnings. 'It's all well and good to speak of forgiveness and peace,' he said. 'But can these Christians really forgive? I think not! I have still to see a warrior turn the other cheek, when he's attacked. And is it honourable? To my mind, a man who proclaims one thing and does another is without honour.'

Beorn nodded thoughtfully. 'But look at Chad,' he protested. 'He was brought here by force, but has forgiven us and become our friend. Is that not impressive?'

'Chad is an exception,' said Penda gloomily.

As Easter-month approached, Beorn announced that he wanted to present his bride to the kingdom of the Middle Angles.

'I shall rule them as a Christian king,' he said. 'Alchfled wishes us to send for Chad's older brother Cedd, soon to be made a bishop.'

Penda shrugged. '*My* children have free will,' he said. 'I gave my word. My word is my honour.'

So messages were sent north and Cedd arrived at the beginning of Gentle-month. He was welcomed warmly by Chad, and courteously by most of the Mercians, but Woden's priest was clearly relieved when he set off for Lichfield in the train of the new king and queen of the Middle Angles.

Egfrid's training progressed and Penda presented him with a rune-marked, pattern-forged sword, specially made for him. It was light in weight and slightly shorter than most weapons, but it was a warrior's sword, fit for a king's son, and Egfrid was proud of it.

'Learn how to use it,' Penda told him.

So Sigurd's training took a new and more serious turn.

Beorn and Alchfled had only been gone a few days when dust rising in the north announced more visitors. Uncertain as to what this might mean, Egfrid and Chad went with the king and queen to meet the new arrivals. Prince Ethelwald and a large party of Deiran thanes rode into the courtyard, their clothes mud-stained and horses lathered, as if they were pursued.

'Ill news, ill news!' they shouted.

'What brings you riding like the Wild Hunt to our gates?' Penda asked.

Ethelwald leapt from his horse, his face flushed and furious. He glanced around the curious, assembled company until his eyes lighted on Egfrid.

'His father...' he cried, pointing at the boy. 'His father has betrayed all honour, all decency and is unworthy to be a king. He has taken Deira from Oswin the Good by treachery!'

Chad stepped between Ethelwald and Egfrid, his hand moving to the hilt of his knife. Penda stared from one to the other, astounded, as did Cynewise. Egfrid's stomach lurched and his courage drained to his boots.

'Whatever the father has done, the boy is not to blame,' the queen said.

'Indeed. Egfrid is still my foster-son—have a care how you insult him,' Penda warned, his voice low and threatening.

But anger blazed in Ethelwald's eyes. 'Wait till you hear what Faint-heart has done! Oswin the Good is dead, and by Oswy Iding's hand.'

'Are you telling us that Oswy has made a challenge for Deira?'

'Oh, he's challenged him, yes, but Oswin did not

have the chance to die honourably in battle. He was murdered.'

'Murdered? How?' Penda demanded.

'In cold blood,' Ethelwald insisted. 'Oswy gathered a great army, with Picts and Scots at his back, and rode into Deira calling on Oswin to hand over his throne.'

'By Woden!' Penda swore. 'What did the lad do?'

'He gathered his warriors together—and I for one went to his aid—but when Oswin saw the size of the Bernician war-host, he backed off, saying he would not fight an unwinnable battle and bring so many of his countrymen to their deaths. You know he has never been a great warrior, but—'

'But he's an honourable man and I put him on that throne,' Penda growled. 'So do you say he ran from them?'

'No. He called for negotiations and took refuge with Hunwald, a local thane, who he thought was his friend.'

'And was he mistaken in that?'

An icy finger of fear rippled down Egfrid's back.

'Utterly!' Ethelwald told his tale with relish. 'Oswy's assassins lay in wait for him, in Hunwald's hall. The Bernicians attacked in the night and all there were slaughtered. Even Hunwald died. Oswy has taken the throne of Deira for himself.'

'Hunwald deserved to die,' Penda spat in disgust. He turned furiously on Chad. 'Is this your king's idea of Christian justice? Is this his Christian peace? The man's without honour. What do you say to this, holy man?'

Chad's face was grim, but he spoke out bravely. 'We are all fallible.'

Egfrid shuddered. Would Penda kill him now? Could his father really have done this vile deed? He remembered only too well his quiet rage, and his desire to rule Deira as well as Bernicia.

Penda gave a sudden roar of fury, followed by terrible silence. Then at last he turned to Egfrid. 'It is not your fault, boy, that you are the son of a traitor. To challenge openly to battle is honourable, but to murder by stealth in the night...it is without honour! All peace agreements are destroyed by this act of treachery.'

There was silence again.

'Call up the army!' Penda roared. 'Ethelwald, *you* shall have the throne of Deira! We march to meet Oswy in battle! Fetch Thunderer to me...my spear and my sword!'

Suddenly it was chaos. Orders were shouted, horns sounded and a steady drum beat started. Men ran in all directions.

'You cannot ride to war!' Cynewise told her husband, her face frantic. 'Beorn must lead them!'

'Do not tell me what I can or can't do, woman!' Penda bellowed. 'Beorn traipses about the country dancing attention on his Christian wife. This is what comes of trusting Christians, and I blame *you* for that! I won't have Beorn ride with me! Send for Wulfhere— he at least cannot be tainted by this coward's disease. Fetch the herb woman with her salves and potions; *she* will get me up and onto Thunderer's back! I shall lead the Mercians. I am their king!'

'Fetch Fritha!' Cynewise sent a servant running.

Penda turned to stare at Egfrid, and for one dreadful moment he feared his last moment had come. 'Get that boy out of my sight and keep him locked up!' Penda bellowed. 'He is my hostage still!'

'Go!' Cynewise hissed to Chad. 'Take the boy to your hut.'

CHAPTER 12

War

Once back in their private space Chad began rolling cloaks into bundles. Dapple bounced down from the bed where he'd been sleeping to lick Egfrid's face.

The boy pushed the hound away. 'What are you doing?' he asked Chad.

'I think we should slip away,' the monk told him. 'Can you carry a bundle?'

'Of course,' Egfrid agreed.

But the sound of feet and the clatter of wood on wood outside made them turn uneasily.

'Who's there?' Chad called.

No reply came. He unfastened the door and opened it cautiously. Two spearheads clashed together in front of his face—two guards had been set there again. 'You cannot leave, holy man,' said one. 'We're sorry, but this is war, we are to bar the door!'

'We're prisoners!' Egfrid said.

Chad let the bundle drop to the floor. He took Egfrid gently by the shoulders and turned him round, making him sit on the bed. 'We've always been prisoners,' he said gently.

'Will they kill me now?' Egfrid asked. 'The king hates me.'

'No, he doesn't hate you,' Chad said. 'He would have sliced your head off there and then if he hated you. But he was furious. This is a terrible moment for Mercia and we must be quiet, calm and patient.'

'*Why* has my father done it?' Egfrid asked. 'Why has he killed his cousin Oswin, and in such a vile way?'

Chad shook his head. 'It is the nature of kingship to be ruthless. Oswin the Good was perhaps too gentle to have ruled for long, and your father was never going to be content until the whole of Northumbria was his.'

Dapple leapt back onto the bed and tried again to lick the boy's face. His tail wagged furiously. This time Egfrid hugged the hound to his chest, grateful for the comfort of one more loyal friend.

The door creaked open and the queen's maid Wyn carried in a tray of food and drink. 'The queen says be quiet and wait,' she whispered.

Chad nodded. 'Thank you.'

Egfrid flung himself down on his bed. 'I cannot be quiet and wait,' he protested. 'How can I be quiet, when they may come at any time to kill me?'

'I will cut a piece of vellum, light a candle and sharpen a quill, and you will write,' Chad said. 'You will copy the psalm of King David.'

So with the sounds of preparation for war all around them, Egfrid wrote, while Chad recited words he knew by heart.

'I will not be afraid of ten thousands,
Who have set themselves against me.'

They spent a restless night, disturbed by the hammering of smiths, the thud of horses' hooves, the shouting of angry voices and the stamp of booted feet. Preparations for war went on through the next day and night. When Chad opened the wooden shutter at dawn on the third day, they saw that the courtyard was crammed with horses and men. Penda's war host was gathering.

Chad set Egfrid to copy psalms again, but half way through the morning the boy threw his quill across the chamber and refused. 'I cannot sit here writing,' he cried. 'I will go mad!'

'Very well,' said Chad. 'Strip off your jerkin and we will wrestle.'

'What? You are a holy man.'

Chad shrugged. 'I can still wrestle.'

'Very well.' Egfrid angrily stripped off his jerkin and rolled up his sleeves. 'I will give you a taste of what Sigurd has taught me.'

Chad rolled up his sleeves and kilted up his monk's habit. Egfrid strode forward and gripped his book-master by the shoulders, but he knew at once that he'd underestimated his opponent, for he quickly found himself thrown on his back.

'Who taught you to wrestle?' he asked, gasping.

Chad laughed, a brief sound of joy in a world that had gone mad. 'I told you, I was the youngest of five brothers,' he said.

Egfrid struggled to his feet. 'I cannot imagine holy Cedd wrestling,' he said.

'Oh, he was the fiercest of all,' Chad told him.

Egfrid came at him again, this time with a little more wariness and respect. They wrestled until they were exhausted and Egfrid felt calmer when Wyn appeared again with more food and drink. 'The queen says, be of good cheer, they will soon be gone.'

With the following dawn came the sound of marching feet. Horns blared, shouts and cheers were raised. Peeping out from the window hole they saw the flap and flare of Woden's raven banners and just for a moment glimpsed Penda, mounted on Thunderer, his leg heavily strapped, his back supported by a leather-covered frame. Egfrid turned away, moved by the sight of the sick, aged king, so determined to lead his men to war.

'I… I have wanted to please him,' he admitted guiltily. 'And I should not have done.'

'You gave him respect, there is no guilt in that,' Chad told him. 'This war is a ruthless battle for land and power.'

As they turned to look again, the great gathering moved off.

'Will they kill my father, do you think?'

'That's in the hands of God,' Chad said.

To the sound of horns and a steady beating drum they set off. The king went first with his hearth-companions, eager for battle, seasoned warriors every one. They were followed by well-disciplined foot soldiers, archers and slingers, each with their own special skills. The local headman led the serfs, ploughmen and young lads, herders and farmers, armed only with axes, pikes, scythes and ploughshares. Unused to fighting, they glanced regretfully back to their wives and daughters. Last of all went the slaves. Unarmed, they led mules and rumbling carts, loaded with food, drink and grain. Egfrid glimpsed Fritha riding amongst a gang of well-wrapped women, mounted on her sturdy pony. He watched her go sadly, for she'd been a good friend to him.

'Some do not look as though they want to go,' he said.

Chad sighed. 'They have no choice, they must follow their lord. Every kingdom that pays tribute to Penda will send the same and when they join together as they move north, there will be many of them.'

'What will my father do?'

Chad shook his head. 'Oswy has already added Pictish warriors and Dalriads to his war host, but I doubt Deirans will go willingly to his cause. Oswin wasn't known as 'the Good' for nothing. He was loved by his people, I think.'

'Damn him…damn my father!' Egfrid cried angrily. 'Will he ride north and hide in the hills, so that Penda may call him Faint-heart once again?'

Chad made no reply and in the quiet that followed the great exit, they heard the murmur of voices and light footsteps approaching. The door was opened and the queen herself stood there.

'I'm so sorry,' she said, and held out her arms to Egfrid. 'So sorry to keep you locked up, but it was for your own safety. I hope you understand.'

Relief that she was not angry made his face crumple as she hugged him. 'I'm sorry too,' he said. 'Sorry that my father has broken the peace that you worked so hard to gain.'

Cynewise nodded. 'Not your fault,' she said. 'I must keep you here, but if you give me your word not to escape, then I will allow you the freedom of Tamworth once again.'

'I give my word,' he said.

They discovered when they emerged that Tamworth had turned into a ghost town. The only men of fighting age were the queen's own warrior band, though at least that meant Sigurd was there. The usually busy workshops were quiet, for the smiths and metalworkers had gone with Penda. Only the gentle clack of working looms rose from the websters' and spinners' huts. The stables stood almost empty, with just three horse-boys left behind. Egfrid was grateful to find Golden-mane stabled alongside Cynewise's silver-grey mare.

The days passed quietly and Egfrid worked with Chad every morning and with Sigurd in the afternoons, but more often he rode out with the queen, who was almost as restless as he was.

'Where is Ranulf?' Egfrid asked, noticing his absence.

'Gone to fight,' Sigurd told him, his face a blank mask.

'I'm sorry,' Egfrid said. 'You must fear for him.'

'I'm proud of him,' the captain insisted.

Egfrid understood.

'Wulfhere and his battle-master will meet the army as they travel north,' Sigurd said.

'And what of Prince Beorn?'

'Beorn must stay where he is and keep well out of this quarrel.'

'Do you wish you could go too?'

Sigurd nodded. 'It is hard to stand back while others

fight, but I stay here to guard the queen...and you,' he added.

Weed-month passed and Harvest-month came and still there was no word of distant battles in the north. Chad and Egfrid went out to help bring in the harvest, turning brown-skinned and weather-beaten. Offerings-month dragged by and even the Night of the Dead passed with few celebrations. In Blood-month the work of slaughtering animals began.

CHAPTER 13
King's Gold

Just as the slaughtering of the beasts began, horses were spotted on the tracks from the north. Was this Penda returning at last? But almost at once they saw that this was just a small contingent with a wagon and few warriors.

'Return to your chamber,' Cynewise told Egfrid sharply. 'I know that banner. It is Wulfhere, with his battle-master Aldred.'

Chad took him by the arm and hurried him away. They watched from their window as a tall lad, well-armed and dressed in mail, rode into the courtyard ahead of the wagon. He was escorted by a small warrior band and an older, battle-scarred man.

'Does this mean they have won?' Egfrid asked. 'Is my father dead?'

Chad pressed his shoulder, but said nothing.

They watched as the queen went to greet her son. He swung her round in his arms.

'I've never seen her look so happy,' Egfrid said resentfully.

'He's her son,' Chad said. 'And she has feared for him, just as your mother fears for you.'

Wyn brought food to their chamber, saying nothing. It seemed a feast took place to which they were not invited, but later that night they were summoned to the hall. Wulfhere sat on his father's chair, one leg thrown over the arm, a horn of mead in his hand, the battle-scarred Aldred at his side.

Egfrid bowed politely and Wulfhere turned a smiling face to him, but the warmth of his expression slipped immediately.

'He's wearing my old hog-skin jerkin,' he said.

Cynewise smiled. 'And why not?' she said. 'He is our foster-son.'

'I have something to show you, Bernician boy,' Wulfhere said, with a sneering smile. 'You may have my old clothes, but I've got your father's gold.'

Egfrid summoned his courage to ask the question uppermost in his mind. 'Is my father dead?'

Wulfhere shrugged. 'Not dead, but disgraced. He ran as he always does when he saw that our war-host outnumbered his. We had the Welsh on our side, Ethelwald of course, and the East Anglians too. We kept your Faint-heart holed up in Stirling castle through the Month of Offerings—and he agreed to pay us three sacks of gold, to go away. Ethelwald will rule Deira now, and I have more Bernician gold in my possession than I have ever seen. Come, I will show it to you.'

Egfrid hesitated, but Wulfhere grabbed his arm and led him from the hall into the courtyard where the stumpy tower that was used as a strong room stood. He lifted the heavy wooden bar and opened the door.

'Come, you will recognise this. You will know where it came from!'

Chad, Cynewise and Aldred followed hurriedly, speaking low to each other.

'You need to see this, Bernician boy,' Wulfhere continued. 'See how your father's courage fails! Let this be a lesson to you for the future: Mercia is overlord.'

Egfrid gritted his teeth. In the light of the torch that blazed from a wall sconce, he saw that the strong room was spread with the glimmer of gold. He could not help but gasp, for Wulfhere was right. The more he looked, the more he saw familiar fragments—broken, all broken and thrown onto trestle tops—sword pommel caps, scabbard pyramids, sword loops, the hilt plates of a seax, but all of them hacked from the weapons they once adorned.

'Ha! I see you come to understand the coward your father is.'

Egfrid wanted to turn and walk away, but pride and a horrid curiosity forced him to stay there looking. He knew how his father valued these riches, these symbols of wealth and power, gathered over many years.

Egfrid's hand strayed towards a narrow dragon's head that once had capped his father's battle helmet with its solemn gold-wrought face. Now the sinuous head was hacked from the body.

'And this—see this.' Wulfhere picked up two broken, highly decorated gold cheek pieces and threw them down onto the trestle. 'Do you know these?'

Egfrid nodded silently.

'And what is this?' Wulfhere snatched up an elaborately worked sword hilt fitting, decorated with garnets and an exquisite curled pattern of twisting creatures.

'It is from my father's sword,' Egfrid said quietly.

'Where is the pommel cap?' Wulfhere asked, rummaging amongst the glittering scraps.

'It's here,' Egfrid said, reaching into the middle of the pile. He drew out the treasured piece that had been made for his father by Frankish goldsmiths and brought by sea from Kent to Bernicia. 'This sword was a wedding gift from my mother.'

Wulfhere laughed nastily. 'Rumour has it that your mother refuses to speak to your father. He dared not ask for her jewel box and instead made his companions hack off their gold fittings and helmet trimmings, which were added to make up the payment demanded of him—three bags of gold. There are two more sacks like this, shared out amongst our allies.'

Egfrid's stomach tightened. It must have been deeply humiliating for his father to be forced to order this crude destruction of the precious gold fittings his followers possessed...but he had brought it upon himself.

'See here!' Wulfhere reached out to snatch up a larger twisted gold plate plaque, fantastically wrought into the form of two eagles holding a fish between them. Egfrid had last seen it decorating Cedric's shield, the one given to him by the young wife who'd died long ago. Cedric would have hated to part with such a treasured possession, but it was the duty of the king's companions to give their all for him—even their lives.

'And this…' Wulfhere went on relentlessly.

From another bag he lifted out what seemed to be a great mash of tangled strips, bent into a strange basket-like shape.

'Look at this, boy, and tell me your father is not a coward! Penda is old and sick, but he straps himself into his saddle and rides to the fight, a true follower of Woden. Your Faint-heart kills by treachery, hides in his castle and buys his safety with the symbols of his faith!'

Egfrid's eyes widened as he suddenly understood what he looked at. It was twisted and crushed, but as Wulfhere prised the strips apart and flattened them, the gold and garnet cross that Oswy carried ahead of his household warrior-band was revealed. How could his father have allowed this desecration of the symbol of his God-given power as a Christian king? Egfrid wanted to crumble into dust at Wulfhere's feet and die. He could take no more.

Cynewise had come into the strong room behind them. 'That is enough!' she said. 'It is dishonourable in you, Wulfhere. The boy is humiliated enough. Chad, take Egfrid back to his guest hut, please.'

'Come,' Chad said quietly.

Egfrid turned and followed his tutor, neither of them speaking until they got inside and closed the door.

'You bore that well,' Chad said at last.

Egfrid looked at his book-master. He spoke through gritted teeth. 'If I should live through this, to be a man, I swear that I will make Wulfhere cry for mercy. I will take every possession he has, and then I will kill him!'

'Go to bed,' Chad said brusquely.

Egfrid threw himself onto his bed and beat the mattress with his fists. He bit the soft woollen covers to stop himself from howling like a wolf. Dapple whined in the corner, sensing his master's distress. Chad watched in silence.

At last Egfrid lay still, exhausted. Dapple jumped up beside him and eventually boy and dog fell into a restless sleep, while Chad knelt upright by the door and prayed all through the hours of darkness.

They were disturbed in the morning by the sound of hooves and voices. When they looked out through the shutter, they saw that the gold was being removed from the strong room and lifted back into the wagon. Aldred supervised and gave orders while Wulfhere hovered in the background.

'What will they do with it?' Egfrid asked.

Chad shook his head. 'I don't know.'

At last the wagon was packed and driven out through the gate in the palisade, Wulfhere and Aldred bringing up the rear. Egfrid heard footsteps approaching and knew it was the queen.

'I apologise for my son,' she said. 'He is young and rash and angry...but he is my son and I would die for him.'

Egfrid, pale-faced and red-eyed, accepted her apology, unsure that his own mother would speak so fervently for him. 'Can we come out again?' he asked.

'You can indeed...more than that! Penda heads back to Tamworth and I will go to meet him. You must come with me, so that I know you are safe. I've had enough of skulking at home while my husband and younger son go to war.'

Egfrid exchanged a brief glance of pleasure with Chad, for he too was weary of Tamworth, and almost anything would be better than being cooped up any longer. 'May I take Dapple with me?'

'Why not?' Cynewise agreed.

'What will they do with the gold my father paid for his freedom?' Egfrid asked uncomfortably.

The queen's look darkened a little. 'I told Aldred to bury it as a gift to the gods,' she said. 'Penda wants nothing to do with it, and I don't want it either. It is not an honourable gift.'

'So nobody shall have it.' Egfrid felt some satisfaction that at least Wulfhere would not keep it.

'The earth shall have it,' Cynewise said. 'Aldred will bury it and tell nobody where it lies.'

CHAPTER 14

Blood-month

They left Tamworth in a patter of rain while thunder rolled in the distance. Despite the threatening storm it felt better to be doing something and Egfrid's spirits lifted. It was good to be out on Golden-mane's back, Dapple racing at his side.

The rain came on more steadily and lashed down on them as they rode towards the high hill passes. Cynewise, wrapped in furs and skins, set a good pace on her silver mare, leaving poor Wyn, wet and miserable, riding behind her.

They made camp on the southern lee of a hill above the River Derwent, but moved on next morning, though thick mist made the going slow. That evening a watery sun struggled out to greet them as they made camp again.

'Where will we meet them?' Egfrid asked, fearful that this brief freedom might quickly be lost to him.

'They'll ford the River Winwaed,' Cynewise said. 'Tomorrow we'll head in that direction and may find them there already.'

The following afternoon they arrived at the southern bank of River Winwaed, only to discover the water-meadows in flood. They made camp on high ground where they had a clear view of the ford. As the light began to fade, Mercian standards emerged from the mist that covered the northernmost riverbank.

'But they cannot cross!' Cynewise protested.

'No, lady,' Sigurd agreed.

'Then we must swallow our impatience and wait till the morning.'

Penda's vast army appeared and settled to camp on the far bankside. Horns blared in greeting from one side of the river to the other and Dapple ran backwards and forwards yapping, as though he recognised the gathering on the other side.

Cynewise waded through mud, almost to the water's edge and Penda gave her a loud halloo. 'At least he knows I'm here,' she said, blowing kisses across the water.

'You'd best go back to your tent, lady,' Sigurd warned her.

Late into the night cheerful shouts drifted across the water. The queen's tents were made of twice-stitched oilskin and though it rained heavily all night, Egfrid was dry and comfortable on the folding bed they'd put up for him.

The next morning he woke to hear Dapple's bark, and struggled bleary-eyed from his tent to find Sigurd on watch. It still rained and a heavy mist filled the valley.

Sigurd drew a sharp intake of breath and Dapple barked again.

'What is it?' Egfrid asked, sensing the man's unease.

'There… I swear I saw something on the crest of the hill, in the mist!'

'A deer…a wolf?' Egfrid suggested.

But Sigurd turned suddenly to him with a horrified expression. 'Damn it!' He snatched up the horn that swung from his belt and blew three sharp blasts.

'What is it?' Egfrid cried.

Then he saw it himself. Moving steadily on the crest of the far hill, a shape appearing from the haze.

'Faint-heart!' Sigurd murmured. Then he blew his horn again and started to bellow. 'The Bernicians are here! To arms! To arms! The Bernicians are on us!'

Egfrid stared into the distance and saw something astonishing emerge from clouds of rolling mist... a shape that he knew well, but roughly hewn from wood, not gold. A cross, linked with a circle: his father's battle standard. Not the fine gold cross that Wulfhere had crushed, but an emblem crudely shaped from green wood.

His heart began to thunder as he stumbled back to his tent. Chad was on his feet at once, as Egfrid snatched up the sword that Penda had given him and began to buckle it around his waist.

Chad said nothing but strode outside. As Egfrid followed him he saw Sigurd leap onto his horse and charge down the hill towards the swollen waters. 'Wake Penda, wake! The Bernicians are upon you!' he cried as he rode into the flooding river.

Cynewise stumbled from her tent in her nightgown, shocked and dishevelled. Wyn followed, clutching her cloak and crying.

'What is happening?' Cynewise asked.

Egfrid could only point to the dark shapes of spears and warriors that appeared over the distant brow of the hill, out of the mist, to swoop down on the unsuspecting Mercians. Chad's face was blank with shock.

'My father,' Egfrid managed at last. 'It is my father; he has given up his gold, but not his swords and spears. Penda is trapped by the swollen river!'

'Go to them!' Cynewise ordered her men. 'Go to my husband's aid! Get your horses and swim them across!'

'Lady, we stay by you!'

'Go!' she bellowed. 'I order it! Follow Sigurd and ride to Penda's aid!'

Her men ran to their steeds, mounted fast and headed for the swirling waters. They could just see Sigurd's horse, carried a good distance downstream. Dapple ran after them, barking excitedly.

'To heel, to heel,' Egfrid cried desperately. Reluctantly the hound returned to him.

'We shall all be killed,' Wyn whispered, weeping quietly.

Sleepy Mercian warriors stumbled from their tents to grab swords, spears and axes, while Oswy Iding and his army rode down out of the mist to kill without mercy.

'Blessed Freya!' Cynewise cried. 'Where is my husband? Wake, brave battle-bear, wake and fight!'

Egfrid felt that his heart would burst with fear.

'Is this fair Christian battle?' Cynewise turned in fury to Chad.

He shook his head. 'I have no answer for you, lady.'

They watched helplessly as Penda's standard was raised. The old warrior could be seen at last amongst his companions, who made a brave stand, but were forced back towards the river, to lose their footing in deep, slippery mud.

'I must fight,' Egfrid cried, his sword there in his hand. 'I must fight.'

Chad gripped him tightly and pinned his arms to his sides. 'And who will you fight for?' he asked.

Egfrid's mind whirled with confusion as he tried to answer. Which side would he fight for? Would he support his cold, calculating father, to whom he owed unswerving loyalty, or the fierce old warrior king he'd grown to love? His father had been ruthless and clever to follow and attack the Mercians here in this flooded meadow, while they slept…but was it honourable?

'Aaah!' he cried out at last, in confusion and agony.

Cynewise clasped his face in her hands. 'Put your sword away,' she whispered. 'Swear to me you will not fight for either man! We must both bear this somehow.'

His mouth was a grim line of pain, but he nodded and sheathed his sword. Chad let him go.

'Where is Ethelwald?' Cynewise cried. 'Why does *he* not come to Penda's aid?'

Egfrid didn't want to watch, but he found he couldn't look away.

The Mercian herdsman's-army had bravely rallied behind the seasoned warriors, but were driven like cattle into the fast-flowing water, only to be trapped in silt and carried away downstream. Cynewise's warband and their horses had vanished in amongst the struggling mass. The queen sent poor weeping Wyn to her tent and told her not to come out again. The woman went readily enough.

'There's Ethelwald,' Chad said, and he pointed to where the Deiran battle-standard had been raised on higher ground. Ethelwald was mounted and rallying his men, but all of a sudden instead of entering the fight, he whirled about and headed further upriver, his men streaming after him.

'What is he doing?' Cynewise cried, her face white and shocked. 'The Bernicians are letting him slip away!'

'But see who comes forward!' Egfrid cried. He pointed down-river to where Sigurd led a large following of warriors through the soaked meadowland.

'The East Angles!' Cynewise cried. 'Sigurd has found King Athelhere and brought him to Mercia's aid. But he comes too late!'

As this new help arrived, Penda's standard was dragged to the ground and the fighting around the Mercian king grew fierce.

The queen set off, rushing down towards the river, just as an armed warrior drove his beast across the raging torrent and through the mire. Egfrid raced after her, feeling only that he must follow where she went. The Bernician rider raised his sword as Cynewise stumbled on, careless of her own safety.

'It is the end!' she cried.

'You shall not touch her,' Egfrid growled and without pause for thought, he lurched in front of her and taking his sword in both hands, he swung it sideways, biting into the warrior's armpit, as Sigurd had trained him.

The Bernician let out a bellow of shock and pain and slumped forwards in his saddle, dropping his weapon at Egfrid's feet. His panicking horse wheeled and charged back into the water to skitter away downstream. Egfrid stared at the bloodied sword that lay at his feet. Had he killed a man?

Chad was there beside them, with Dapple leaping up and down. The monk gently pulled Cynewise away and began to lead them both back up the hillside. 'Come away, lady,' he told her firmly. 'There is nothing you can do.'

'He is gone,' she murmured softly. 'Penda is dead, I saw him fall, the bravest warrior that ever lived!'

Egfrid picked up the Bernician's sword, his first spoil of war, and followed them back up the hill. As they reached the queen's tents again, Cynewise turned angrily on him. 'You should have let me die,' she said. 'I would have gone with him. You swore you wouldn't fight.'

'I swore I wouldn't fight for my father or Penda,' Egfrid said. 'I never said I wouldn't fight for you.'

The queen's face crumpled and she flung her arms around the boy and wept. Egfrid remembered the fateful ride from Bamburgh on Thunderer's back, the moments of unexpected joy when the grizzled old king had praised him. He could not believe that such a valiant, fearless spirit as Penda was gone. He felt sick and angry, but he was elated too. His father was no faint-heart. Nobody could ever say that again. Oswy had paid off the enemy with gold trimmings, but kept most of his spears and blades and his fighting spirit intact.

CHAPTER 15

Woden's Man

The Bernicians, cheered on by Ethelwald's desertion, drove the remnants of the helpless Mercian army into the flooding river, and then put all their force into tackling King Athelhere.

It was not a fight any more. It was a drowning, for the ground beneath the East Angles' feet had turned into a swamp of dragging mud. As Egfrid and the queen watched, they saw one man swim steadily across the river towards them. He battled against a strong current, but made it to the field below and came loping up the hill towards them. It was Sigurd, soaked and slashed with bleeding cuts, choking on muddy water.

Cynewise shook her head. 'You should have gone down with Penda,' she said.

'No,' he gasped. 'Penda died sword in hand, a true Woden's man, as he would have wished, but Athelhere too is killed and the kingdom of Mercia is no more. I swore on oath that I'd take you to safety.'

Cynewise shook her head fiercely. 'No, it is Wulfhere that you must save,' she said. 'He is camped near Lichfield with Aldred. Take my horse and ride to them and warn him. Hide him. *He* is Mercia's hope. Beorn will have to do as Oswy tells him now.'

'Lady, you must come too,' Sigurd begged.

'Yes, you should go with him,' Egfrid added his voice. He found he couldn't bear the thought of her being captured.

But Cynewise refused. 'Wyn can go. Where is Wyn?' she asked. 'I stay here to see my husband's death rites. My fate is in the three dark spinners' hands.'

Sigurd looked at Egfrid. 'The boy is your hostage,' he cried. 'And though I love him, by rights he should be killed. Lady, they have cut off your husband's head!'

Wyn cried out, emerging from the queen's tent.

Egfrid gasped in shock at Sigurd's words, but he hauled together every scrap of courage he could muster. 'I am willing to die,' he said. 'My father has killed your husband, lady, and by the rules of blood-feud it is just. I'm no faint-heart.'

They stared at him. Vomit suddenly rose in his throat, and he staggered away from them a few steps to be sick.

Chad strode to his side. 'If you must die, so shall I,' he said quietly. 'The boy will not die alone.'

But Cynewise shook her head. 'There will be no more killing,' she said firmly. 'This boy saved my life, using those very warrior skills that you yourself taught him. No, Sigurd. Take my horse and ride fast to Wulfhere. I order you to do it as captain of my guard—you are my man still. Take my mare and ride away with Wyn. You must both serve my son now.'

At last Sigurd bent to kiss the queen's hand, while Chad threw a saddle over the queen's mare and led her forward. Wyn scrambled up behind Sigurd and they rode southwards, back towards the high ridge of hills.

The queen, the monk and the boy, stood together in silence, as the dreadful sounds of dying men reached them from the far riverbank.

'What will we do?' Egfrid asked at last.

'We cannot do anything till the waters go down,'

Cynewise said. 'We wait for now. I will see you safely back to your father and in return I shall beg that he allow my husband Woden's rites.'

Egfrid knew the importance she placed on this, but he doubted that his father would be generous. Oswald Whiteblade's body had been hacked to pieces and staked out for a raven-feast.

They gazed across the river at a scene of utter devastation. Bodies floated downstream, though many of them were caught in reeds and rushes at the water's edge. On the far hillside, Bernician warriors walked from corpse to corpse, stripping weapons and cloaks from dead or dying Mercians. Here and there it seemed the water ran red with blood.

'Did our Christian God want this?' Egfrid asked.

Chad shook his head and the boy saw traces of tears on the monk's cheeks.

Darkness fell and the three of them kept watch all night, sitting close together wrapped in furs. The rain ceased, but the night was cold and none of them could sleep or eat. Dapple curled close to Egfrid, sharing warmth, while the queen wept quietly for her husband and her warrior band.

'You could still ride away,' Egfrid told her, as he

stroked the hound's silky ears. 'Take Golden-mane. I will not stop you, nor will Chad. I doubt my father knows that we are here. I'll even give you Dapple, if you want him.'

But she shook her head. 'My son is safer if I'm not with him,' she said. 'And if I hand you back, at least I'll feel that I have done the honourable thing.'

Chad offered words of Christian comfort to the queen.

'Hush,' she told him. 'Woden is my god and Freya my goddess, like Penda. My loyalty stays with them.'

As light came, they saw that the Bernicians were wading into the water to drag bodies back onto land. Cynewise vanished into her tent to emerge a short while later, looking very much the queen again. She'd combed her hair and dressed herself in a clean gown and cloak, and she'd set a fine gold fillet at her brow.

'Come,' she said. 'We cannot sit up here for ever.'

So they wandered down towards the crossing, leading two horses, Dapple trotting at their side. Some Bernicians watering their mounts near the ford looked up at their approach, and stared as though they'd seen ghosts.

Egfrid strode forward. 'Get my father!' he shouted. 'Tell Oswy Iding his son is here.'

They looked confused. 'Oswy's son?' they murmured. 'But he was taken hostage. Surely he cannot still live!'

Someone was sent running and at last Oswy himself came striding down to the river, blade in hand, his face pale and gaunt, a long gash on his cheek. Ribbons of leather hung down from a makeshift sword hilt, the fine blade of the weapon still intact.

He stopped, looking astonished. 'Egfrid?' He closed his eyes. 'God be praised,' he said, still sounding dazed. 'My son is alive.'

Egfrid helped Cynewise mount Golden-mane. Chad mounted his horse and hauled Egfrid up behind him. They approached the ford, which was still deep and running fast, but managed to get across.

The queen dismounted and waited for Egfrid to slip down from the saddle. She took him by the hand then and led him to his father with great formality.

'I, Cynewise, foster-mother to Egfrid of Bernicia, do give your son back to you. I kept him safe as I promised to do. And your holy man too.'

Oswy and his companions stared, speechless and astonished.

Then Cynewise threw herself down onto her knees, careless of the mire. 'Allow my husband Woden's rites. That it is all I ask of you.'

Oswy's eyes blazed and his face turned paler still. 'What of my brother's Christian rites?' he asked.

She made no reply.

Egfrid hated to see the queen kneeling there in the stinking, bloodstained mud. 'Cynewise is a woman of honour and she is my foster-mother. Give her the boon she begs!' he cried.

Oswy stared at his son, utterly surprised. 'Where is my gold?' he asked. 'And where is the boy Wulfhere? Do you think I can let him live?'

Cynewise moaned gently.

'Father, your gold is buried. Given to the ground by a man who will die rather than reveal its whereabouts. That same loyal man hides Wulfhere too.'

There was a moment of tense silence. Oswy raked his fingers through his dirty hair as though he was tired and puzzled by it all.

'My son went away a boy, but it seems he returns a man,' he murmured. Suddenly he smiled and it was as if a watery sun had broken through dark clouds. 'You shall have your pagan rites, lady,' he said. 'And so shall

all the Mercian dead. Despite my many sins, it seems the Christian God has blessed me.'

He dropped his sword, held out his arms and hugged Egfrid tightly.

'My son has come back to me,' Oswy said. 'And that is better by far than gold.'

AUTHOR'S NOTE

The exciting discovery of the Staffordshire Hoard, made by metal detectorist Terry Herbert, provided the inspiration for my story. My intention is to give an idea of life in the 7th century, and the sort of story that might lie behind the hoard. Rival kings fought fiercely over territory—and yet sometimes they sent their sons and daughters to marry their bitterest enemies in an attempt to make peace. The Venerable Bede refers to a payment of gold in settlement of a dispute:

At this period King Oswy was subjected to savage and intolerable attacks by Penda, King of the Mercians who had slain his brother. At length dire need compelled him to offer Penda an incalculable quantity of regalia and presents as the price of peace, on condition that he return home and cease his ruinous devastation of his kingdom.

Bede also mentions Egfrid: 'Oswy's son Egfrid was at the time held hostage at the court of Queen Cynewise in the province of the Mercians.' Egfrid was about ten or eleven years old when Penda was killed. How he became a hostage is not known—so my story explores the more exciting possibility of his capture, rather than his father handing him over to the Mercians. Bede records a raid on Bamburgh, when Penda attempted to burn the fortress, but was foiled when the wind changed direction and blew the flames back onto the attackers. Egfrid survived to become king of Northumbria on his father's death in the year AD 670.

Anglo-Saxons often called their children by names very similar to their own, which makes telling a story from that time quite difficult. Penda's oldest son was called Peada, but I felt that would be too confusing, so in the story I have given him a nickname: Beorn, meaning bear.

The Staffordshire Hoard is on permanent display around the UK. Find out more and see pictures at *www.staffordshirehoard.org.uk*.

Theresa Tomlinson
Whitby, June 2014
www.theresatomlinson.com